THE HOLLYWOOD MURDERS

A Golden Age Mystery

G.G. VANDAGRIFF

Dedicated To

Elizabeth "Buffy" Faith Vandagriff Bailey
for her brilliant content editing

and

for being the daughter every mom dreams of

Chapter One

1935

Mid-Atlantic fog draped over the ship like a shroud as Catherine and Harry took an evening walk on the deck of the Queen Mary. Sailing on the new ocean liner to America from England was a luxury neither had experienced. The ghostly night yielded few sounds except those of the sea clapping against the hull. Under their feet, they felt the reassuring vibrations of the ship's engines. Harry pulled Catherine into his arms to steal a kiss.

Angry words reached them out of the heavy mist, "*Sie hat es nicht getan!*"

Catherine heard a thump. Was the speaker pounding the handrail? Turning to Harry, she whispered, "That's German. What is he saying?"

"' She didn't do it.' He sounds pretty heated up about something," Harry said.

As they approached, the speaker materialized in the fog. He was alone, wearing a coat and hat and leaning dangerously forward against the ship's rail. Apparently, his words were meant only for the sea.

Alarm flashed through Catherine. *Is he going to jump?*

"Excuse me, sir. Do you need help?" she asked, her voice muffled by the fog.

The figure turned to face her. Whisking off his hat, he bowed. "Excuse me, madam. I didn't mean to trouble you. Pay no heed to me."

"But," said Catherine, pressing him. "You are very upset."

"I am very disturbed, but it is nothing to worry you over."

"I don't like you being disturbed when you are so close to going overboard," she replied.

"Ah. But it is not I who am in danger. It is my daughter, you see."

He turned back to the rail, his anger evident in his rigid stance. Harry looked resigned when she went to join the man. His hat covered the stranger's thick gray hair once more, and he clutched the handrail like a lifeline.

"Perhaps it would help if you talked to someone," Catherine said gently.

The rail shuddered as he hit it again. "My Dafna has been accused of murder."

Harry sighed. Catherine winced. They had both had their fill of murder. How did it find them in the middle of the ocean?

But Harry gently took the man by the arm and said, "Come and have a drink with us at the bar."

* * *

The three of them sat in barrel-shaped chairs in the Art Deco lounge. Now that Catherine could see him in the light, she was surprised to realize that the man was not as old as she had thought from his posture. His dark hair was only slightly touched with gray, and his handsome face was scarcely lined. The man had an Old-World air about him with his correct European tailoring and formal manners. He had introduced himself as Dr. Gerhardt Adler from Vienna.

He drank a Schnapps while Harry had whiskey and Catherine a glass of tonic water. "Is your daughter with you?" she asked.

"She is in America. California. I am on my way there now," the professor said.

Catherine was hardly even surprised at the coincidence. "So are we," she said. "Dr. Bascombe and I are going to teach summer courses at the University of California in Los Angeles."

"Ah! But this encounter grows even stranger!" the doctor said. "I go to teach there as well."

"What is your subject?" asked Harry. "We are English literature professors."

"Ah!" the man said again. "I teach the psychology."

Catherine saw the interest kindle in Harry's hazel eyes. He was exceedingly fond of the subject. Before they could begin a discussion of the science, she asked, "And your daughter? Is she a student?"

"No. She is an actress on the cinema. They call her Daphne Binoche. Perhaps you have seen her work?"

This news stunned Catherine. She exchanged glances with Harry. Daphne Binoche was a gifted French actress and quite famous. "Yes. She is brilliant. I never suspected she was Viennese."

"It is no secret, but the French are very possessive. She made her career there, and the country has embraced her, so to them, she is French. I took this post to be near her," the professor said. "And now this has happened."

"How dreadful. Perhaps it would help you to talk about it. We are very discreet," said Catherine. "I can tell that it weighs heavily on you."

"I think, if I do not impose, I would like to tell someone about my Dafna's troubles. I am growing mad with keeping them inside. I am chewing on them like an old horse with no teeth. I have the headache that will not go away."

"How perfectly dreadful," said Catherine, feeling for the man. She knew what it was like to have a member of her family suspected of murder. "Feel free to tell us. You are traveling alone?"

"Yes. You are so kind." He leaned forward, his elbows on the table. "Of course, Dafna was not able to tell me much in her telegram. She just asked me to come earlier than I had planned for the autumn semester. You see, she has been questioned concerning the murder of her director. I only hope I am not too late to help her." He shuddered and ran a shaky hand through his hair. "The only things I know about him come from her letters. If you are a devotee of the cinema, you may have heard of him. He is called Michael Fields."

"I have heard of him," said Catherine. "He produces and directs suspense films, doesn't he?"

"Yes. He did." The professor pulled a pack of letters from his pocket tied up with string. "These are Dafna's letters. From them, I learned that Mr. Fields was from a well-known family in Chicago. His father was a manufacturer of steel. He was very wealthy."

He took a deep breath. "Dafna does not like his wife, and his wife does not like her. This has caused problems. There are two grown children," he said, smiling briefly as he shrugged. "You see since her mother has died, I have become her confidante."

Catherine and Harry exchanged glances. She didn't wish to appear insulting, but she wondered about the nature of his daughter's relationship to the victim. She had heard of the "casting couch."

As though reading her mind, Dr. Adler said, "I have wondered too if they were lovers, but I do not know the answer. You understand she would not confide such a thing to me, her Papa. She only said that he was brilliant and that she could not believe the chance she had to work with him. He went all the way to Paris to find her and to convince her to go to Hollywood to star in his film."

"Perhaps there is a jealous boyfriend," suggested Harry.

"I have also thought of this. Dafna's leading man is called Buckingham Danforth. It seems a silly name to me, but what do I know? Dafna calls him Buck. I hope she will confide in me when I arrive."

"I've heard of him, too. Maybe others in the production have motives," suggested Catherine. "I shouldn't think you need to worry so much. Perhaps one of the actors had a grudge. There must be plenty of suspects."

The professor leafed through the letters he had placed on the table. Pulling out one, he unfolded it and read it through quickly. "Yes, this is the one. It was written three weeks ago. Allow me to read it. 'Michael has been very . . . upset. There are problems on the . . . set." At this point, the professor said in an aside, "Is that what you call it in English?"

Catherine nodded.

He continued. "'Buck is being difficult, and Ruth' . . . that is his wife . . . 'is creating dramas. And to . . . crown it all off, Michael's son, Del, appeared on the set demanding money from his father! We have not filmed one scene this week.' That is the last letter I received. The telegram about the murder arrived three days before I departed from Vienna. Since then, I have been miserable with worry. I know nothing about these American policemen. Will it be like Austria? Will they take against my Dafna because she is Jewish?"

The anxiety behind his words smote Catherine. She had heard disturbing tales about the treatment of the Jews in Austria and Germany. And she would have to be blind and deaf not to notice the problems with anti-Semitism in her own country. It was all most unsettling. Ever since becoming Chancellor two years ago, Hitler had fanned the flames with his diatribes about the superiority of the "Aryan" race.

"I don't know anything about the police in America," Catherine said. "But I don't think they would ever admit to such a thing. America isn't Germany or Austria. But perhaps Harry and I know one or two things about working with the police. Maybe someday we can tell you more about that, but in the meanwhile, I suspect we could make a little discreet inquiry about the matter if you like."

"It would be good to know. I would appreciate it," said the professor. "You have been very kind to listen to an old man. Tell me more about yourselves. What is your university?"

Harry said, "Miss Tregowyn teaches at Somerville College, the women's college at Oxford. I'm at Christ Church."

Catherine gave a short laugh. "We are academic rivals, of course."

"You must have an interesting marriage."

"Oh! We're not married," said Catherine. "As a matter of fact, here comes our other traveling companion!"

Catherine's greatest friend, Dot, joined them at the table, looking a bit green. Catherine reached out to squeeze her moist hand. The professor and Harry stood.

"Dot, this is Professor Adler. Professor, this is my friend, Miss Nichols."

The professor gave a perfunctory smile and nod. "It is a pleasure to meet you," he said.

Dot smiled a smile of significantly reduced wattage than usual. "You must forgive me, Professor. I'm not feeling at all the thing. Turns out I'm a rotten sailor."

"You're not feeling any better?" Catherine asked.

"The ship's doctor gave me something. I'm feeling marginally better. Enough better to want a G and T."

"I'll get it," said Harry. He rose and went to the teakwood bar.

"The professor is going to be teaching at UCLA this autumn," said Catherine. "Quite a coincidence." She turned to their new friend, "Dot is in advertising. This is a business trip for her."

"Splendid!" said the Austrian.

When Harry returned a moment later, bearing Dot's drink, he told her that the professor was a psychologist.

Harry asked if he was acquainted with Sigmund Freud, and they spent the next half hour listening to the professor's personal dealings with the father of his science. Then, noting that Dot was looking worse, Catherine offered to return with her to their cabin.

They took their leave of the men and went to their shared stateroom with its black and white Art Deco furnishings and side by side beds. Catherine was grateful to be sailing on the newly commissioned ship with its stylish atmosphere and fabulous service. Their beds had been turned down with foil-wrapped chocolates left on their pillows.

"I'm sorry you're so sick," she said to her friend.

Dot tried to be cheerful. "They say it won't last once I get my sea legs."

Once they were tucked up in their beds, Catherine said, "Well, not a day has passed since Southampton, and we've already come upon a murder investigation."

"Crikey! Who was murdered?"

"Michael Fields, the director. You've heard of him, haven't you? It happened in Hollywood."

Dot said she did know the director. "How horrid!"

Catherine told her friend about the professor's daughter's involvement and his concerns. "You'll never guess! His daughter's Daphne Binoche!"

"You've just banished my seasickness! Tell me details!"

Catherine told her what she knew. "I didn't want to appear a ghoul. We didn't ask too many questions. We just listened to his concerns. But we've already got a list of suspects—Fields's wife and two children, the leading man, and other members of the cast."

"Well done," said Dot. "You've given me something to think about besides the ship's rocking. Daphne Binoche! Fancy! Do you suppose we'll get to meet her? I never thought we'd actually come across any film stars on this trip. Not really. But one hopes."

"The professor is worried about the police being anti-Semitic. We're to put our ears to the ground and find out what the situation is. Poor man. He's desperately worried, and it'll be days before we can get there."

"Well, I've no doubt that Providence put Dr. Adler in our path for a reason," said Dot.

Catherine and her best friend had already been concerned with three other murders in the last year. It seemed fantastic to her that they might have stumbled upon another one.

"Hold on, Dot. There's no reason to think that Daphne Binoche will want us involved in her personal business."

Dot just responded with a sigh.

Chapter Two

The next day was stormy with high winds. Unfortunately, Dot was so ill she told Catherine she didn't dare leave the cabin.

She and Harry spent the day playing chess, darts, and talking further with Professor Adler about his work in Vienna. Harry told him of his own work attempting to psychoanalyze the Victorian writers.

"Of course, I'm just an amateur and haven't anything like your knowledge," Harry said.

"I would be interested to hear some of your ideas," said the doctor.

They began discussing Thomas Hardy, whose fatalistic stories were so intriguing to Harry. "He struggles to find a reason for the human condition," said Harry. "He wants to put a face to fate."

"But are not all good writers that way?" asked Dr. Adler. "It seems that is the task they give themselves when they take up the pen."

Harry responded, "And none more so than the Victorians—they needed to explain the universe."

Catherine said, "The post-War writers certainly aren't that way. They seek to expose the brutality of life and the utter capriciousness of fate."

Dr. Adler was a dedicated Socialist, which led to the discussion of politics and the human psyche. Hitler, of course, was a prime example.

"You must excuse me," he said. "I've gotten on what the Americans call my 'hobby horse.' You are very kind to listen and to try to take my mind off personal affairs."

They were sitting in one of the lounges at this time. People were gathered in groups all about them, conversing, laughing, and drinking a great deal of gin. Women were dressed in imaginative day gowns, which Catherine knew were created by the best designers. Men wore elegant lounge suits and smoked pipes and cigars. A string quartet played in the background, and well-dressed waiters circulated with trays of canapes.

At one point in the conversation, when Harry had become quite passionate about his dislike of Dickens, an extraordinarily lovely woman passed in front of their little table. Harry stopped mid-sentence and stared at her. As though feeling his look, the beauty turned and gazed at him for a moment, jerked up her chin, and then quickly moved away.

Harry fell to knocking out his pipe in the ashtray with some violence. He didn't finish the point he had been making, concentrating instead on refilling his pipe. Catherine could see that his hands weren't steady.

Who is that woman, and what is she to Harry?

Catherine wished Dot were there. Her friend knew everyone in High Society, if not in person, then through the London society pages. The incident punctured Catherine's well-being. Occasionally, she had wondered about Harry's past. Here it was. He had some sort of history with that woman.

The lady now sat on the other side of the lounge, and though Harry's back was to her, Catherine had an excellent view. She had a long, lean look and wore her blonde hair pulled back in a chignon, revealing an aristocratic profile—high cheekbones, a delicately defined jaw, and a perfect nose.

Catherine knew her own looks to be very different with her brunette hair worn short and fashionably finger-waved. Her large brown eyes were set in a heart-shaped face. She suddenly felt very pedestrian.

"Who is that woman, Harry?" she asked.

"Which woman are you talking about?" he replied.

The professor looked from one of them to the other.

"You know who I mean," Catherine insisted. "She caused you to forget what you were saying and attack your pipe."

"She's just someone I knew eons ago. I was surprised to see her, that's all."

"Does she have a name?" asked Catherine.

"Lady Naomi Wadsworth."

Catherine recognized the name. Lady Naomi had caught the imagination of society. Her doings were legend. She could fly a plane. She shot big game in Africa. She had taken a First in Modern Languages at Somerville. Catherine couldn't help but know the name, but she had never met the woman. They moved in vastly different circles. Catherine was a poet, a tutor, and a minor aristocrat, but her circle was relatively small. Lady Naomi was a Liver of Life on a large stage. Catherine couldn't believe she hadn't recognized her from the newsreels.

Out of deference to the professor, she decided to leave her many questions for later. Instead, she suggested they play a game of hearts. The professor agreed enthusiastically, Harry less so.

* * *

"Do you know Lady Naomi Wadsworth?" she asked Dot when she returned to her cabin to dress for dinner.

"Slightly," said Dot. "She goes about with fast company, but occasionally she has drinks with Charlie, and he has introduced us."

Charlie was a feature writer for *The Times* and Dot's friend from The Spotted Pig, a Fleet Street pub she frequented after work.

"Do you know if she and Harry were ever an item?" Catherine asked.

"No idea," her friend said. "Why?"

"She walked by us in the lounge, and he reacted very strangely. The sight of her put him completely off his stride."

"Hmm," said Dot. "I would say they were around the same age. Perhaps they knew each other at Oxford."

Catherine pulled a red evening gown over her head. Dot did up the buttons.

"What is your impression of Lady Naomi?" Catherine asked her friend.

"She's not the warmest of creatures as far as her own gender goes. She was lovely and attentive to Charlie."

"I can't abide women like that," Catherine said as she powdered her face. "I wonder what she's getting up to in America."

"Something newsworthy, I imagine," said Dot. "You know, I really think I might try dinner this evening."

Catherine beamed. "Come, I'll help you get ready."

* * *

The seas had calmed by the time Catherine and Dot made their way to the dining room. Harry was not yet at their table when they arrived. They studied their menus.

Catherine was trying to decide between roast beef and lamb chops when Dot leaned over to say, "Harry's over at Lady Naomi's table. Speaking to her."

Catherine's heart pounded sickeningly at the news.

"How does he look?" she asked her friend.

"Angry," she said. "Oh, now he's coming over here. He's absolutely seething."

But when he greeted Catherine with a kiss on the cheek, he seemed perfectly normal, except for the slight flush on his face. "I've asked the professor to join us tonight to make a fourth."

"Lovely," said Catherine automatically. She studied Harry as he sat next to her and unfolded his napkin. He seemed the same as he always did. She'd had no idea he was such an expert at disguising his feelings. The thought was unwelcome. How was she to know when he was sincere?

Dot took the bull by the horns. "I saw you talking to Lady Naomi a minute ago. What amazing thing is she up to now?"

"She's going to visit the place they call the Grand Canyon, then she wants to experience Hollywood. Turns out her bosom friend is Daphne Binoche."

Catherine felt a twinge of anxiety. "What a coincidence," she said, striving to make her voice light. "Oh! Professor Adler. How nice that you could join us."

"Good evening, Miss Tregowyn. Miss Nichols, I must say you look much improved. It is good the storms are behind us."

"I am feeling much more the thing," Dot said. "Tell me, Professor, will you fly or take the train to Los Angeles?"

"Oh, I will fly, most definitely. I must get to my Dafna as soon as possible. What about you?" Professor Adler asked.

"I will take the train, I think. Though I must stop in New York City for the first week. I have business there," Dot told him.

"Oh!" The professor looked intrigued. "And what is your business, if I may ask?"

Their waiter came at that moment to take their orders. Everyone had decided on the lamb chops. The remaining courses—soup, salad, and dessert—were set.

Dot continued, "I have two purposes while I'm in New York. My advertising firm has set some appointments with ad agencies there, so I can see what sort of thing they are doing in the States. I'll be looking for new ad markets for my agency's clients, as well as scouting out new American clients for our agency. But I am also trying to find investors for a little business of my own that I hope to start in London. English lotions, soaps, bath powders, that sort of thing. I'd like to eventually ship to the American market."

"I am impressed!" said the Professor. "You are an entrepreneur. My daughter will enjoy meeting you. She is a self-starter, as well. Going into the cinema is not easy for a woman. There have been many hazards."

"However did she manage it?" asked Dot. "She is a raging success."

The professor brightened at the question. "She studied acting in Paris. She was on the stage there and eventually worked her way into films. Mr. Fields—the man who was recently murdered—saw one of her films, went to Paris, and offered her a contract if she would move to Hollywood. It was a big decision to make. She was doing very well in France. But in the end, she decided to do it, against my objections. I did not want her so far away. And now look what has happened. Mr. Fields has been murdered, and she is a suspect." He wiped his forehead with his napkin. "It is all I can think about."

Catherine put a comforting hand on his wrist. "You will be there soon. Isn't it marvelous that we can fly from New York in just 18 hours?"

"Yes," the man said. "I should have become an idiot sitting on a train for all those days."

"Tell us more about your daughter," Catherine invited the Austrian after the dinner plates had been removed and the coffee served. "What made her decide to become an actress?"

"It was always her dream, but she knew she would have to study in Paris, and she didn't want to leave her mother. They were very close. More like sisters than mother and daughter. My wife was ill for the last two years of her life." The professor removed a pipe from his pocket. "Dafna moved to France after her mother died.." Dr. Adler filled his pipe from his tobacco pouch. "It was a terrible wrench for me to lose them both one right after the other."

"She must speak English if she is going to be appearing in an American film," said Dot, sipping her coffee. "And your English is excellent, as well."

The professor tamped down his tobacco. "My wife learned English as a child. She was Russian, and her father was a diplomat. He insisted she learn English, French, and German. Daphne and her mother were both very gifted with languages. We had months where we would speak nothing but French. Then the next month, nothing but English."

"I am guessing that your wife was a beautiful woman," said Harry.

Dr. Adler laughed. "Of course! It is obvious Dafna did not take after me! Those eyes! They are her mother's eyes. Lavender."

"Extraordinary!" said Harry, organizing his own pipe. "There is one thing I don't understand, Herr Doktor. You mention that you worry about the police mistreating Daphne because she is Jewish. How would they happen to know her religion?"

"Ah! An excellent question. You see, Dafna was something of a radical when she lived in Paris. There, politics are more extreme than in Britain or America. There is overt Fascism. As you know, the Fascists hate the Jews. Dafna was very active in the Anti-Nazi movement and even became a Communist. Her religion became known. I expect if they know their job, the American police have checked with the Sûreté in Paris. Dafna was involved in some illegal demonstrations. She was arrested. No doubt her religion is part of her record. In France, it would be."

"I see," said Harry. He drew on his pipe. "Well, perhaps we can find out whether or not that is part of the Americans' profile of your daughter. Offhand, I would say her Communism may be more troubling for them than her religion."

* * *

After dinner, Dot and Catherine had tickets for a film showing in the ship's theatre. Harry assured them he would entertain himself happily. The professor wished them a good evening.

To their surprise, the women discovered the film was Daphne Binoche's latest. Since it was in French (with subtitles), it had obviously been made before the actress's move to Hollywood.

"What luck!" said Dot.

"Too bad the professor didn't know about this," said Catherine. They settled in to watch. As soon as Miss Binoche's face appeared, Catherine felt a childlike thrill. Who wouldn't think she was the world's most beautiful actress? Her dark hair cascaded over one side of her face and across her shoulders. Well-marked eyebrows gave character to her large, light-colored eyes, which in the opening sequences sparkled with fun and laughter. High cheekbones and a full, wide mouth defined her face. Her teeth were perfect.

Catherine was enthralled. She could not believe that she would meet and talk to this glamorous woman in a matter of days. Her captivation was so complete she didn't even follow the film. Instead, she studied Miss Binoche—the way she moved, laughed, flirted, and cried. She hoped most sincerely that the woman wasn't guilty of murder.

Chapter Three

The final days of their voyage were only remarkable for the utter relaxation Catherine experienced. She saw Lady Naomi here and there, but Harry seemed oblivious to the woman now.

By the time they reached New York City, Catherine was ready to be on land again. Standing on deck as they came into the harbor, she was profoundly moved by the iconic Statue of Liberty. Catherine was neither poor nor oppressed, but she could imagine how it must have looked to those who were—particularly the victims of the Great Potato Famine. Solid. All-embracing. Full of promise.

She gripped Harry's hand. He squeezed it back.

They enjoyed a day in New York, staying in the luxurious New Yorker Hotel, seeing a matinee of the American musical, *Porgy and Bess*, and dancing into the wee hours to the hotel band. It was all tremendous fun.

In the morning, Catherine and Harry said goodbye to Dot, who was off to her first appointment. Despite Catherine's coaxings, Dot declared herself not brave enough to fly alone across the country. She had elected to take the train to meet them in Los Angeles. Catherine thought her very brave to go ahead with her business, traveling alone in a foreign land.

"I'll give Max your regards," said Catherine with a smile.

"He's to meet us at the airport. Meanwhile, the best of British luck to you."

"Good luck to you with those American students!" Dot got into the waiting taxi and slammed the door.

* * *

Catherine took one look at the big DC2 TWA airliner, and all the confidence she had felt because of her short flight in Rafe's six-seater left her. The wings were enormous, with massive engines hanging from them. And it was so big! How could it possibly stay in the air?

The trip was to take eighteen hours with three stops. That meant four take-offs and four landings. Anxiety clawed at Catherine's stomach and caused her heart to race. As she climbed the stairs to the door of the craft, she nearly slipped. Throwing out a gloved hand, she caught herself on the rail. The stiff wind blew off her little hat, and she watched it cartwheel across the tarmac.

"Oh," said Harry. "Bad luck. I'll go chase it for you," he offered.

"No. I need you right where you are. It's just a hat," Catherine said.

When she was aboard, Catherine looked at the fourteen seats—navy blue with red and white TWA logos on the headrests. Taking a deep breath, she smiled at the female attendant who welcomed her aboard while examining her ticket. She heard thumps below her as the luggage was loaded into the hull of the airplane.

Suddenly there was an immense roar. Catherine's eyes rounded in terror until she realized it was the sound of the aircraft's engines starting up. The whole plane shook as though it would disintegrate into pieces.

You can do this. You can do this. You can do this.

Catherine's hands grew clammy inside her gloves.

"You're in the second seat on the right," said the attendant.

Catherine slid into her seat, swallowing a lump of pure terror which had arisen in her throat. Harry was across the aisle from her. As he took off his hat and laid it on his lap, he gave her a thumbs-up signal and a wink. She wished she were sitting on his lap with his arms holding her tightly. She closed her eyes and concentrated on counting to one hundred.

A speaker sounded in the aircraft cabin.

"This is your flight captain. Welcome to TWA Flight 200 to Los Angeles. Our first stop will be in St. Louis, where we will refuel. You will be able to deplane there, and a hot lunch will be awaiting you in the coffee shop. The flight will take about five hours, so I hope you had breakfast. Our attendant will be passing out chocolate bars mid-flight. There may be a little rough weather, but nothing we can't handle. I hope you have a pleasant flight and enjoy flying with us on Transworld-Western Airlines."

* * *

By the time the airplane made its third stop in Denver, Catherine was exhausted and hungry. The dinner was steak—a big, thick steak. The menu called it "Western-style."

"Isn't Colorado the state where Max is from?" Catherine asked Harry. Max was the UCLA exchange student who had studied with Harry during the last Michaelmas term. He and Harry had put together the program that Catherine and Harry were now to teach at his college. Max was an oddity--a cowboy with a thirst for Nineteenth-Century British Literature. It had never made sense to Catherine.

"Yes. But he's not from Denver. He grew up on a ranch where they raised beef like this."

The young man had also had a fling with Dot, and Catherine knew her friend had been more than a little disappointed when Max wrote of his engagement to his long-time American girl-friend.

"I don't think I will ever be able to hear properly again," said

Catherine. "Am I shouting? Those engines are so loud my ear-drums are numb."

"I imagine when we fly over the Rockies, your ears will get blocked up from the extra altitude. I wish it were daylight so we could see the mountains," said Harry.

"Nighttime is all right with me. I'm not as fearless as I thought. Who would have imagined a country could be so big! It just goes on and on!"

Harry reached across the table and took her hand. "You're doing marvelously well. Admit it! Isn't it better than spending days on the train?"

"It will be when it's all over, I suppose," Catherine said. "But you love it, don't you?"

"I am a bit. Speaking of planes, I can't keep from wondering, how is Rafe getting along," Harry said.

When will he ever stop asking about Rafe? " He's tremendously bucked up about my brother's African drinking water project. I'm so pleased that he's helping to finance it. That means the world to Wills."

"Will he ever return from Kenya, do you think?" Harry was trying to sound casual, but Catherine knew he was bluffing it.

"Not until the British authorities have forgiven his crash land-ing in the Thames."

Harry got the brooding look his face always wore when they discussed her former boyfriend of long-standing. He was like a man who had lost a tooth and kept probing the spot with his tongue though it always pained him.

"Do you think he's reformed?" asked Harry.

She gave a sigh of impatience. "From what I understand, all it takes is one drink for Rafe to head downhill again. While I wish him well, I'm not interested in taking any more chances where he's concerned. You know that, Harry. Why do you keep worrying about it?"

"You know why," he said dryly. "I'm not about to go into it in a public dining room."

20

"Well, if you don't want to discuss it, then don't ask about him," she said, her voice sharp.

* * *

It was midnight when the airplane landed for the last time. Catherine let loose a terrific sigh of relief. It felt like she had been holding her breath since leaving New York.

The blond, blue-eyed, and freckled Max met them at the airport, complete with cowboy hat. "Welcome to L.A.," he said. "I'll bet you're exhausted. I sure was when I made the flight last December."

"It's really good of you to meet us," said Catherine. "How far is it to UCLA?"

"Well, we're not in L.A. proper," he said. "We're at the Burbank Air Field. That's where most airplanes fly these days. There's an airport hotel not too far from here. It's not glamorous, but I thought you might want to stay there tonight, and then tomorrow we can make the drive to Westwood, which is where UCLA is."

"That sounds heavenly," said Catherine. "Perhaps by then, I'll have my hearing back."

* * *

The hotel was by no means glamorous, but Catherine scarcely noticed. She went straight to sleep after having a quick wash. When she awoke in the white room the following day, she had no idea where she was.

The walls appeared to be whitewashed rather than painted. The windows were set into the foot thick walls. The art was bright-colored and primitive, and the floor was covered with woven mats of something suspiciously like straw. But there was a large en suite bathroom, as she had noted the night before, containing ordinary soaps and towels.

Catherine showered and washed her hair. One of the switches on the bathroom wall turned on a novel overhead heat lamp that helped her hair dry quickly.

It was difficult to gauge the outside temperature, but she decided it would probably be hot. She was further south than New York. That was the only thing she was sure of. After donning a somewhat wrinkled linen dress, she left her room to begin discovering California.

Harry was sitting reading a newspaper in the colorful lounge. "Sleep well?" he asked.

"Like a baby. You?"

"The same. And I can even hear this morning. I have explored somewhat, and there is a place called Rosa's next door that does breakfast."

They walked next door to a humble building—white with turquoise trim. A waitress with long flowing black locks and a large red flower behind her ear showed them to their seats. Her "uniform" was a white, off-the-shoulder blouse tucked into a full skirt that must have had half a dozen petticoats under it.

Catherine realized this was a tribute to the Mexican influence she had read about. California was part of Mexico when it was under Spanish rule.

"A lot of Mexicans live here," she said quietly to Harry. "Did you notice that our hotel was built like a Mexican casa? Those paper mache things hanging from the ceiling must be piñatas. I read about them. They are full of candy. Children break them open with poles on their birthdays."

"How do you know so much?" Harry asked.

She held up her guidebook. "I came prepared. I read up on the cruise. One of the other things I learned is that Mexican food is very spicy, so watch out. Remember you have a British palate."

Harry perused the menu. "I'm going to try the Mexican egg dish. I can't pronounce it, but it sounds great."

"Dot would love this place! I'm going to try the eggs, too. Oh! And look. They have fresh orange juice."

The eggs were delicious, served with avocados and something called sour cream. Max walked in just as they were finishing.

"*Hola*! *Amigos!* I am so glad you discovered this treasure of a café. Did you have the *huevos rancheros?*"

"We did, thanks," said Catherine. "They are delicious. I was just telling Harry how much Dot would like all of this."

For a moment, he tightened his lips. Then he said, "I thought she was coming with you." His eyes were unreadable. Catherine wondered if his fiancée was in L.A. or back home in Julesburg.

"Dot'll be along later. She's in New York at the moment."

He smiled broadly. "Good! Well, are you ready for your journey to Westwood? That's where UCLA is. Close to all the poshest hotels and restaurants and houses. But you'll find it very different than what you're used to. This is desert. We have to pump our water in from the Colorado River. So it's not very green, I'm afraid. Some places are landscaped, but they have to be irrigated. New York was cosmopolitan, but here you're really going to feel like you're in a foreign country."

Max was driving a large touring car. Catherine hadn't registered it the night before. "This car belongs to the college," he said. "It's for driving our important visitors around."

Nothing could have looked more different than New York or England. They drove down roads that looked newly paved with asphalt straight through neighborhoods of bungalows, none of which looked older than twenty years. Some had lawns, but most were just surrounded by dirt.

The Depression had clearly hit here. It wasn't hard to find the signs of poverty—dilapidated houses, boarded-up businesses, and ill-dressed children playing in the streets.

Finally, Catherine saw evidence of the city that must be Los Angeles in the distance, but it had only a few multistoried buildings and no skyscrapers like they'd seen in New York. They didn't go through it but instead stopped short by a large tract of brown dirt, crowned by a new building that looked to Catherine to be built of golden sandstone. It had an expansive green lawn, and two bell towers, on either side of the main building. There was a long, lower building along one side of the large new one.

"This is the University of California at Los Angeles," said Max. Catherine felt a vast disappointment. She hadn't expected Oxford, but she had expected a decent-sized university. Was this the best one of the largest cities in California could do? How and why had they imported her and Harry? And Professor Adler with his impressive credentials?

She must have communicated her feelings somehow to Harry. He moved his hand across the seat and gripped hers tightly. "Chin up," he mouthed.

Max also must have felt her mood up in the front seat. "Different than Oxford, eh? Don't worry, a University is more than its building. We have some excellent faculty. And important donors. The plan is for a much larger place. If you come back in 10 years, you won't recognize it. There's a lot of money in Southern California, despite the Depression. There's oil, you see. And wait 'til I show you where the film stars and the movie moguls live."

"Have you met Professor Adler yet? From Vienna?" asked Catherine. "He came over with us on the ship. I think he flew out here the day we docked."

"Yes. I picked him up at the airport, too. You'll be putting up at the same inn in Westwood Village."

"Oh, I am glad," said Catherine. "He's a lovely man. I shall look forward to getting to know him better. He studied with Freud, you know."

"Yes. It's a tremendous coup for us to get Dr. Adler. He said his daughter lives here, so that was the draw, I suppose," said Max.

By this time, they had arrived in the hamlet of Westwood Village. It was a cluster of white buildings, palm trees, and patches of lawn, unlike any other village she had known.

"Why is everything painted white?" she asked.

"It's the Spanish influence. They constructed their buildings of adobe bricks and then white-washed them to reflect the heat away. We don't use adobe—which is little more than mud and straw—but we try to imitate the look. That's also the reason for the tile roofs."

"Yes," she said. "I remember reading about adobe. What I didn't really appreciate was the heat!"

"Yeah. Not like England, that's for sure," said Max.

He had drawn up to a low roofed inn with the requisite red-tiled roof and a colonnade of arches behind which were red-painted doors.

"This is your inn," Max said. "I think you will find it very comfortable. You will each have a bedroom, bathroom, and a sitting room. Good desks have been provided with adequate lighting."

They were in the act of unloading their luggage from the car when a door flew open, and a distressed Professor Adler ran out of his room.

His words were a muddle of German, and he waved his hands in the air. Harry's German came to the rescue.

"Miss Binoche has been arrested," said Harry with a tired sigh. "He wishes us to go with him to the jail to see whether she is being ill-treated."

Catherine went to the professor and put a placating hand on his arm. "Try to calm yourself. We will come with you as soon as we are able." She turned to Max. "Have we appointments this afternoon?"

"You have one this morning with the Dean of the English Department. He wants to welcome you and tell you what's what. Also, he'd like to go over your syllabus. Then lunch is on at the employee dining hall with resident faculty."

"Did you hear that, Professor?" Harry asked. "We will be available early this afternoon. We'll meet you here at about 1:00. I know this must be tremendously upsetting, but you can't let your daughter see you like this. I suggest a cold shower and a walk. You can familiarize yourself with the town. Find the bookstore, pharmacy, and that sort of thing."

Max intervened, "Miss Tregowyn and Dr. Bascombe may be able to help you. They're good that that sort of thing. When I was at Oxford last year, there was a murder. The police had arrested the wrong man. In fact, they arrested three different people before Miss Tregowyn found the right person. It was someone the police never suspected."

The professor looked at them with wonder. "You solve crimes?"

"Well," Catherine said. "It's not our principal work, but we have managed to help the police a few times." Was she ready to spend the time she had looked at as a holiday chasing down another murderer? She had to admit the professor's distress was wringing her heart.

"But this is wonderful!" said the professor. "Will you help my Dafna?"

"It might be a bit difficult," said Harry. "You see, we know none of the people involved."

Dr. Adler's face fell. "Well, you must at least meet my daughter and listen to her story."

"Yes," said Catherine. "We can do that."

She worried about the professor all the way back to the university and their appointment with the dean. Fortunately, that went smoothly. He welcomed them heartily, gave them a map with their rooms indicated, and told them a rental car was at their disposal. When he gave them their office keys, Catherine began to feel a little bloom of excitement at this academic adventure.

Chapter Four

When they were reunited with the professor that afternoon, they found him to be even more nervous than he had been that morning. His face was pinched with worry, and his hair standing up where he had been running his hands through it. But he had on a finely tailored suit, freshly laundered shirt, and a navy silk tie.

Catherine advised him gently to comb his hair, and without further ado, they left. Having asked the hotel desk clerk for directions to the Lincoln Heights Jail where Daphne Binoche was being held, Harry drove there with a minimum of difficulty in their new Chevrolet Master automobile. It was a beautiful motorcar with a long front end, a lovely chrome grille, and a running board. Catherine felt like she was driving in a Bentley.

As far as Catherine could tell, Los Angeles was notable only for the tall white tower of City Hall. It was nothing like New York. A red streetcar ran along its Broadway while a throng of pedestrians walked to and from the few multistory office buildings.

The weather was hot. Except for on the beaches in the South of France, Catherine had never felt anything like it. And, unfortunately, she was not in her bathing costume.

When they finally arrived at Lincoln Heights Jail, Catherine's heart quailed. It was not the place for a famous film star. She couldn't even imagine what the professor must be thinking. The building was a stark cement block, coated with coal dust. Grim in the extreme.

Black linoleum covered the floor of the reception room. The walls were painted an institutional dull green, and the man barricaded behind the reception desk was cheerless.

"We're here to visit Miss Daphne Binoche," the professor said. "I am her father."

"And the people with you?" asked the police officer.

"Detectives," Professor Adler said without missing a beat.

"Our facilities will only allow you to meet with the prisoner one at a time."

The police officer rang a bell sitting on his desk. A soberly dressed woman guard with a firearm on her hip appeared and proceeded to search Catherine. First looking through her purse, the guard then patted her down. Catherine found the action wholly offensive. The guard gave the police officer a nod, and he let both Catherine and the woman through the barrier. A tall, gangly uniformed policeman similarly searched Harry and the professor, and they were let through. All three of them had to sign a register.

The tall officer led them through the building's dim recesses and up the staircase to the first floor. An overwhelmingly sour, unpleasant odor assailed Catherine. They were shown a bench to sit on.

Professor Adler went in first. Harry and Catherine sat on the uncomfortable bench. She said, "This is horrid."

"What did you expect?" asked Harry.

"I can't think of the woman I saw on the screen being kept in a place like this."

"Hopefully, it won't be for long. If the police allow Miss Binoche to be out on bail. I certainly hope she will be allowed a solicitor."

"They called them lawyers over here, I remember reading," said Catherine. "At least it isn't damp in here. If we were in England, the whole place would smell of mold."

"One advantage of the desert air, I suppose."

They had been waiting for about a quarter of an hour when a handsome fellow wearing what was undoubtedly an Italian suit was shown in by another officer. With him was a short, balding man with a large fleshy nose, also well dressed.

They were all silent, studying each other covertly. Catherine thought the man in the Italian suit must be an actor. He had thick, black wavy hair, held in place by Brilliantine, deeply set brown eyes with heavy, long lashes and expressive eyebrows. His movements were studied. An air of professional good looks surrounded him as sure as any uniform.

When at last the professor came out, Catherine stood up and went inside. She felt exceedingly anxious.

The room was bisected by a wall of barred windows above a counter separated into spaces with stools. Visitors perched on the stools. Prisoners sat on the other side of the bars.

"You are the woman my father was telling me about," the actress said as Catherine seated herself. Her voice was not as heavily accented as Catherine had anticipated.

Even behind bars, the actress looked surprisingly beautiful in her khaki-colored uniform. Her hair waved naturally to her shoulders, and her lavender eyes were clear, though shadowed with fatigue. She moved her head and hands as though she were on film.

"I'm Catherine Tregowyn, Miss Binoche. Please call me Catherine."

"I wish I could shake your hand," the woman said. Even in prison, she managed a commanding presence.

"What has your father told you about me?" Catherine asked.

"Just that you are from Oxford and have solved some . . . crimes." Miss Binoche drew into herself on the last word.

"Yes. Your father would like me to help you, but I must confess, I know nothing of how these things are done in America. I just arrived."

"Oh. Then you cannot help me?" All at once, that commanding

presence was gone, and she seemed to shrink. Catherine's heart squeezed.

"Sometimes, an outsider's view can prove helpful," she said. "Do you have any idea who killed Mr. Fields?"

Miss Binoche once again sat up straight. "I think it was his wife. She thought we were having an affair."

Catherine waited for her to go on.

"We were not," the actress said.

Catherine smiled. "There is a very handsome man who wears Italian suits and has wavy black hair waiting to see you."

Her eyes grew large. "It must be Buck. You have met him?"

"I just guessed he was here for you. We didn't speak."

"You must meet him!" The woman's eyes brightened with hope. Her accent deepened in her excitement. "He can introduce you to everyone. Do you think you can prove that Ruth Fields did it?"

Catherine wet her lips. "Suppose my friend, Dr. Bascombe, and I just look into it. We may be able to help. But I can't promise anything. You might be better off hiring a detective."

"No, no. You do not know these people. They are frightened of bad press. They would never talk to anyone like that. They will never talk to the police. The cast . . . well not Buck, but all the others . . . I think they want me to admit that I did it, so there will be no trial. Then they can forget it and *voila*! They go on with their lives. But there will never be another director like Michael." Tears filled her eyes. "I came to America to work with him. I would never have left Paris for anyone else. He was magic."

"What else can you tell me about him?" Catherine asked.

Miss Binoche's eyes took on a distant look. "He was one of those people the English say was 'larger than life.' He always got his own way." She pinched the bridge of her nose between her thumb and forefinger. "He did not understand the word 'no.'"

"He sounds like he was quite a presence," said Catherine.

"How could he be murdered? Wherever he is now, he is probably outraged," said the actress.

"He had a temper?"

"Oh, yes. A horrid temper. He always had to be in control. I escaped those rages, but other people were not so lucky. Ruth lives in Manhattan most of the time. She's a stage actress there. Her people have lived there before the Indians, I think."

"Ruth is his wife?" Catherine asked.

Miss Binoche ran her finger between her collar and her neck as though it were too tight. "Yes. And there are two impossible grown children, Del and Alvira. Del and his father hardly speak, and Alvira has an unfortunate boyfriend who wants to be an actor. I don't know them well. They are students at the university."

"UCLA?"

"Yes."

"I am teaching there this month. Do you have any idea what they are reading?"

The woman gave a little huff of impatience. "How would I know what books they are reading? I do not see what that tells us!" she said, her voice sharp.

Ah! Michael Fields was not the only one with a temper! "Sorry. That was a British term. I meant 'studying.' That would tell me if there is a chance I might see them at University."

Suddenly the woman was weeping. "I'm sorry to be so short-tempered. Forgive me. This is all . . . it is all too much."

"I don't even know how the murder was committed," said Catherine. "Can you tell me?"

Miss Binoche wiped at her tears with her fingers. She stiffened her spine. Catherine admired her fortitude. This had to be diffi-cult.

"We were at his apartment, and someone knocked. He went to the door, and the murderer shot him right through the heart. He threw the gun down beside him. My gun. I discovered him and called the police, but I didn't notice the gun. All I could see was blood. I learned about the gun afterward. I thought I could save him . . . it was all so horrible and fast. One moment, he was answering the door, and the next moment he was dead!"

31

She wept so bitterly, Catherine decided she was too distraught for any more questions. She handed Miss Binoche a clean handkerchief. "I am sorry you are so distressed. It will be good for you to see your friend. I will send him in." Catherine stood.

"Thank you," Miss Binoche said, using the handkerchief to wipe up her face and blow her nose.

* * *

"Buck" was chatting to Harry and the professor when she entered the visitor's hall. Catherine introduced herself and told him the actress was waiting to see him. He was off like a shot.

"Her lover, I think," said Professor Adler.

The short man with the fleshy nose had risen at her entrance. Now he gave her his hand. "Phillip Westerman," he said. "I have been retained by Mr. Mayer to represent Miss Binoche."

Catherine shook his hand. "Will they let her out on bail, do you think?"

"Mr. Mayer is determined that they will, and his word has a lot of clout in this town. The arraignment is set for tomorrow, and then she should be out of here."

"Mr. Mayer? I'm sorry. Should I know who he is?" Catherine asked.

"One of the movie moguls. Metro Goldwyn Mayer. MGM is his show. He's Miss Binoche's producer," Mr. Westerman said.

Catherine felt a weight lift from her shoulders. Miss Binoche was being looked after. That should make the professor feel better. "Well, I'm glad about that," she said.

Professor Adler had risen as well. "I am glad that you are representing my daughter. If there is any question of a fee . . . "

"Mr. Mayer is taking care of all of that," said Mr. Westerman.

With this information, the professor's countenance brightened, and she saw him shed what seemed to be years of worry.

Harry shook the lawyer's hand. "Best of luck to you." Turning to Catherine and the professor, he said, "Let's go get a cup of coffee somewhere. This place is making my skin crawl."

"I need to wait until Miss Binoche's friend comes out. She said he would introduce us to his circle," Catherine said.

"If you're going to mingle with Hollywood types, I feel I should warn you to be careful of the press," said Mr. Westerman. "They are on this like water on a duck's back. They followed Mr. Danforth here, and they'll be waiting outside the jail with their cameras."

Catherine realized then that they had walked into a drama of enormous proportions—a millionaire movie mogul, a beautiful actress, her handsome lover, and a murder. Even she knew "movie star journalism" was formidable, so of course, the press would be involved.

"They won't know who we are," she said with more confidence than she felt.

"Some police snitch downstairs might have told them that the professor is Binoche's father."

"Oh, dear. Well, let's hope not."

Apparently, Miss Binoche was anxious to meet her lawyer, for it wasn't long before the handsome actor returned to the hall. He told the lawyer she was waiting for him.

Harry introduced Catherine to Daphne's friend, Buckingham Danforth.

"Daphne was impressed by you," he said. "She told me to take you around to meet everyone."

"Yes," said Catherine. "Hasn't the filming stopped at this point?"

"Fields' assistant is carrying on, and there are scenes to film without Daphne. I don't expect she'll be in here long. Mayer's taking care of it."

"We're staying at the Westwood Inn," said Harry. "You can reach us there." Taking out one of his calling cards, he handed it to the man.

"You can be sure I will," Buck Danforth said. "I'll do anything I can to help Daphne. Are you free this evening?"

"We are," said Harry after exchanging a look with Catherine.

"Meet me at the Starlight Club on Sunset Boulevard. I'll leave your name at the door. I'll have at least a couple of the crowd with me."

"Thank you," said Catherine. "We will see you then."

She took the professor's arm, and they left Lincoln Fields prison for what she hoped was the last time. They had scarcely exited when bulbs flashed in their faces, and eager young men asked, "What can you tell us about your daughter Mr. Adler? How are her spirits? Will she be getting out on bail? When will that be?" Turning to Catherine, they said, "Who are you? What is your relationship to the prisoner?"

Harry tried to shield the professor with his much taller form and said, "Dr. Adler has no comment. We have no comment." The professor, who seemed shell-shocked by all the flashing lights, allowed himself to be pulled along to the Chevrolet. The reporters followed, still taking photos until their little group was safely inside the car.

"Well, that was unpleasant," said Harry when they had pulled away.

"Is anyone following us?" asked Adler.

Catherine looked out the back window. "No. They are waiting for Mr. Danforth, I'm sure."

Harry, who seemed to have oriented himself amazingly well, drove them back to Westwood. The professor was quiet, looking at the uninspiring view.

Chapter Five

When they arrived at their destination, the professor said, "I noticed a Jewish delicatessen down this street on my walk this morning. It's called Sol's Spot. Could we go there? I'm sure they have coffee, and I missed lunch."

Catherine was intrigued by the idea of a Jewish delicatessen. The first she had heard of such an establishment was in New York. It was unprepossessing on the outside, with cuts of meat and sausages in the front window. Inside, strange but delicious smells greeted her. They sat at a wooden table, and a waiter wearing a white tablecloth tied around his middle gave them paper menus with the special of the day and other items. She didn't recognize most of them.

"I'm peckish," she said. "Do they have anything like tea cakes?"

"There's strudel," said the professor. "Apple and blueberry."

"What is strudel?" asked Catherine.

"It's a sweet, light dough with a fruit filling, usually sprinkled with sugar. There's an art to a good strudel," the professor told her.

She ordered the apple, Harry ordered the blueberry, and the professor ordered lox and bagels with cream cheese. They all ordered coffee.

Catherine was transported. The strudel was marvelous.

"Your daughter is a strong woman," she told the professor. "And with Mr. Mayer backing her, I think she will be out on bail soon. I can only imagine how difficult it must have been to see her in that jail."

"Mayer is Jewish," said the professor. "One of the wealthiest men in this part of the world, I understand, but I hope that does not hurt her case with the jury. And her lawyer is Jewish, too. I am beginning to realize this is a kind of Jewish community. In Eastern Europe, it would be a ghetto. Here it is a place of wealth and influence."

"I think you're right," said Harry. "I don't think you need to worry about anyone persecuting your daughter."

"But you will still look into it?" asked Adler, "Or do I ask too much?"

"Miss Binoche would like me to. I promised I would," she told the man who was eating his strange sandwich. It turned out bagels were buns with a hole through the middle, and lox were salmon slices.

"Did your daughter have anything useful to tell you?" Catherine inquired. "Anything that could help us?"

The professor put down his sandwich. "She did reassure me that despite efforts on Fields' part, there was not and never had been any affair going on between them. She says she is only friends with that man she calls Buck."

"He is charming in a movie-star sort of way," said Catherine.

"Dafna says there is a lot more to him than what appears on the surface. He has his own secrets, but she won't reveal them, even to me. Maybe I imagined it, but it seemed to me she was nervous when she talked about him. She wouldn't look in my eyes."

"That's intriguing," said Harry. "Will you come with us tonight to the Starlight Club?"

The professor laughed humorlessly. "I think I would get in the way. An old person like me."

Harry did not press him. Catherine thought the professor was right. People would not reveal anything negative about his daughter with her doting father present.

*　*　*

Catherine attempted to rest that afternoon, but it was so hot that even with the fans blowing, she could not sleep. Finally, she took a cold shower and sat in her slip at the vanity table, where she tried to do something interesting to her hair. Cherry, her maid, had given her some tips before Catherine left for America, but she felt she was all thumbs. Setting it in pin curls was the easiest thing. At least her dark brown hair was shiny with a natural wave, so she had that advantage.

What did one wear when one was going to a nightclub to mingle with movie stars?

She had not considered that question when she was packing, but the overly enthusiastic Cherry had. She had a sequined black frock with a Mandarin collar that left her shoulders bare. It ended at mid-calf. It was not terribly imaginative, but she comforted herself that one could hardly go wrong with classic lines.

*　*　*

Sunset Boulevard was lively with neon-lit movie theaters, lounges, and restaurants. Harry helped Catherine out of the cab. He was dressed very nicely in a white dinner jacket, showing off his dangerous good looks. Despite the warm night, she shivered at the touch of his kiss on her cheek. She kissed him back.

The Starlight Club was dim inside, with light coming from the floor, cast upwards along the dark blue walls studded with silver reflective "stars." To Catherine's delight, the music was smoky jazz. A "bouncer" bulging out of a full tuxedo took their names and checked his list with a pencil torch. When he found them, he bid the waiter standing next to him to show them to Danforth's party.

Catherine and Harry made their way carefully across a dance floor to a table covered in white linen and candlelight. Buck smiled a welcome and stood when he saw them. Putting his hand on the bare back of his companion, a brittle-looking blonde dressed in white satin, he said, "Hyacinth, these are the people from England I was telling you about—Harry and Catherine."

The girl gave them a brilliant smile as though she were posing for a photograph.

"You probably recognize her," Buck confided. "Her stage name is Hyacinth St. Clair."

"Kisses, darlings," said Hyacinth. "We are so glad you are here to help us through this scrape. Our poor, dear Michael." And then she was suddenly wiping tears from her cheeks.

Catherine disliked her on the instant. Belatedly, she noticed another person at the table—a man who made her vaguely uneasy. He stood as she saw him and held out his hand. "Joe Calloway."

Her hesitancy fled. "Joseph Calloway!" Catherine exclaimed with delight, shaking his hand. "You were Mr. Abernathy in that thriller last year. You made my blood run cold."

Buck spoke, "He really is a very comfortable sort of guy."

Calloway was black-haired with heavy black eyebrows and a pencil mustache. His eyes were curiously light. "Cursed with the face of a villain," he said.

Catherine and Harry laughed.

"Come, take a chair," said Buck. "I was just telling these two about my visit to Daph."

"How do you two know Daphne?" asked Mr. Calloway.

"I only met her today," said Catherine. "But Harry and her father became fast friends on the ship when we came over."

Harry said, "He's a brilliant man. Studied with Freud."

Calloway appeared uninterested in the professor, instead zeroing in on Catherine. "May I presume on our short acquaintance and ask you to dance?" the man asked.

"Of course," she said, rising to her feet.

The tune was a slow one, and it felt strange to be in the arms of someone who was not Harry. At least that is what she told herself, as he held her a little too tightly.

"So how is our leading lady doing in the slammer?" he asked.

Startled by his animosity, Catherine said. "Have you always played villains?"

"I haven't the face for anything else. Besides, I enjoy it. If you won't talk of our dear Daphne, tell me: where do you come from in England? What brings you to our fair shores?"

"Harry and I are from Oxford. We're here to teach a summer course at UCLA. It was only coincidence that brought us together with Professor Adler. He's teaching there, too."

He raised his formidable brows. "Is that so? Well, because I liked you immediately, I must warn you. You'll want to steer clear of our dear Hyacinth. She has a habit of showing up in print. She's being quoted about this thing everywhere right now," he said. "She loves it."

Throwing a glance at their table, he said, "There's a radio personality who deals in gossip. He's likely to turn up here any time. An obnoxious lout. Has a faux British accent that should amuse you. His name's Richard Darcy. Or rather, that's his stage name. I suspect his real name is something like Sam Stubbs. He's all over this story."

"But surely one of the aims of this club must be to keep the press out?" Catherine said.

"Oh, he's a celebrity these days. His radio show is syndicated coast to coast. Buck tells me you are looking into this. What's your angle? Why were you at the jail if you don't even know Daphne?"

Catherine felt a dart of alarm. She should have expected his curiosity. She detected an edge to it, however. *Best tread carefully.* "The professor is our friend. He's afraid that his daughter is going to be a scapegoat because she's a foreigner," Catherine said.

He gave a mirthless laugh. Before she could go on, he said, "A Jew, you mean?"

His words gouged her. "Possibly," she said. "I can't say I blame him."

"This place is a Jew town," he rasped. "They have their long noses in everything. Bunch of Shylocks."

Catherine wasn't interested in an anti-Semitic rant. Uncomfortable, she manufactured a slight stumble. "Oh, how clumsy of me!" she said. "I seem to have turned my ankle."

Joe Calloway was immediately contrite. "My fault. I'll take you back to the table. Lean on me."

She gave what she hoped was a convincing wince. They hobbled across the room. Harry wasn't there, but Buck stood in alarm. "What happened?" he asked.

"Just clumsiness," said Catherine. "I turned my ankle. Nothing serious."

"Let me get you a brandy," he said.

"No need, really," she protested, sinking into the padded bench seat of their large booth.

"No trouble," Buck said, and he was gone.

She saw that Harry was dancing with Hyacinth and tried to relax. At least the jazz was good. There was a Negro crooner on the piano and a fabulous saxophonist.

Catherine remarked, "The music is wonderful." She looked around her. Classic Calla lilies in silver vases stood on all the tables. Everyone was in full evening regalia. Jewels twinkled under the lights. Obviously, this was the place to be seen.

Mr. Calloway must have noticed her regard, for he said, "They get the best here at the Starlight. This is the place to come."

The number ended, and Harry returned with a pouting Hyacinth. "Darling," he said. "I saw you limping across the dance floor."

"Just a minor mishap," Catherine said. "I turned my ankle."

"Bad luck!" he said. "Let me get you a drink."

"Mr. Danforth has gone for one," she said. "See? Here he is."

Hyacinth said, "Such a fuss!"

Catherine thanked Buck and accepted the drink. She detested

brandy. To her, it was like medicine, but she forced herself to take a sip. It burned all the way down, and she couldn't help a slight choking cough.

"Easy does it," said Buck. He turned to Harry. "I know Daphne thinks you can help her, but I'm at a loss to know how. Did you perhaps know her when she was in Paris?"

Catherine was glad it was Harry who was expected to answer.

"No," Harry said. "We became quite well-acquainted with her father when we were aboard the Queen Mary. He heard from a friend of ours at the university that we had helped the police in a few investigations in England. He jumped to the idea that we might be of help. Since we know none of the people involved and haven't the least idea how your police operate, I don't think we will be able to help much, however."

Catherine could feel Joe Calloway's eyes on her.

Buck said, "Well, the police have the wrong idea entirely in this case. They seem to think Daphne was a spurned lover of Michael's. I imagine they were put on that track by Ruth, Michael's wife, or perhaps one of his children. They hate Daphne. Ruth's always been convinced there was something between her and Michael, but there wasn't."

Hyacinth said, "I wouldn't go that far if I were you, darling. I'd swear there *was* something between them. A woman always knows."

Joe Calloway barked with laughter. "You only say that because he never fell victim to your pathetic charms."

Catherine realized she was coming to dislike the villainous actor more heartily by the moment.

"I think there must be more to it than that," said Catherine. "Spite by a spouse is surely not enough to get a woman arrested!"

"Her little bitty gun was found at the scene," said Hyacinth. "Right next to the body. What more do you want than that?"

Buck said, "I bought the gun for her. They're more common-place here than what you're used to in England. I've never been happy about the area where she lives. It's rather rundown. But she likes Mission-style architecture. Coming from Paris, she finds most of L.A. 'bogus,' she says."

"Unfortunately," Joe Calloway added, "the gun's pretty distinctive. Little pearl-handled thing. She carried it in her purse."

Catherine had thought when she was with Daphne that the woman was innocent. Now she wondered if even Buck had his doubts.

Hyacinth had apparently had enough of all this talk. She said, "Harry, darling, I would love to dance again. All this talk of the murder is so depressing. I miss Michael dreadfully."

Harry looked at Catherine, who gave him a slight nod while keeping a straight face. Harry evidently felt the young woman to be a trial.

They got up and moved out on the dance floor. Hyacinth cuddled up to him. Catherine bit her lip to keep from giggling. Poor Harry!

"She's not as much of a dimwit as she makes out," said Buck Danforth. "I have never met anyone quite as calculating."

Catherine turned to him and asked, "So, I assume you're Miss Binoche's leading man in this picture?"

"I am," he said. "And Joe here is the villain, of course. It gives him great satisfaction to strangle Hyacinth."

Catherine thought it all sounded very predictable. "There must be some kind of twist in it, or it wouldn't be a Michael Fields picture."

"We're sworn not to tell," said Calloway with a laugh. "We've signed the Hollywood version of The Official Secrets Act."

"I wonder that Miss Le Claire can keep a secret!" marveled Catherine.

"Oh, she doesn't know the end," said Danforth. "Michael didn't trust her an inch."

Catherine laughed. "How can she not?"

"She has a restricted version of the script. She's the victim and leaves the scene early. Don't tell her she doesn't have the real script, for Pete's sake," said Danforth.

"Will the picture really go on?" asked Catherine.

"Bound to. Papa Mayer has a bundle tied up in it," said Danforth, who was drinking a martini. "Daph is going to get out on bail, and there is an assistant director—John Hale—who will carry on with Michael's vision for the film. He'll probably be a big success on his own one day."

"Ah!" said Catherine. "Motive!"

Buck smiled his heartbreaker smile. "He was at the beach with his family when it happened. He has half of Santa Monica as witnesses."

"Hmm," Catherine said. She wished she had something else to sip.

When Harry and Hyacinth had returned, a gangly man with a fringe of blond hair around a shining pate and a nose that had obviously been broken once approached them. "Good evening, Buck! You have guests? I have never met these lovely people before."

The labored British-like accent was a dead giveaway. Catherine realized this must be the radio gossip personality.

Buck Danforth stood and shook hands. "Richard. As always, it's a pleasure to see you."

Catherine realized she was seeing Buck Danforth's acting ability firsthand. Of course, the gossip was probably the least welcome person he could imagine, but you would never know it from that greeting.

"These are visiting professors from your home country—Miss Catherine Tregowyn and Dr. Harry Bascombe. Catherine, Harry, meet Richard Darcy, a Hollywood radio host.

"How do you do, Mr. Darcy," said Catherine. "Tell me, where do you hail from?"

"Oh, here and there," said Darcy airily. "London and places north."

His accent was unlike any Londoner she had ever heard. It was clearly an unskilled American attempt to be British. Though uninvited, he sat down and ordered a martini.

"What subjects do you teach, Miss Tregowyn? Dr. Bascombe?"

Harry spoke. "I'm Nineteenth-Century Brit Lit. Miss Tregowyn is Twentieth- Century, but she's also a poet of some renown."

"Ah! Fascinating! I absolutely adore Charles Dickens! Are your classes open to the public? I should like to take one in if I can fit it into my schedule."

"Actually, we're both giving a couple of seminars each week," said Catherine. "But we'll also be doing weekly lectures open to the public."

"Excellent!" He handed over his business card. "Perhaps you could telephone my secretary with the times and the venue. I'll give it a plug on the air. It's just the kind of thing my listeners might find entertaining. We're starved for culture in these parts."

To his right, Buck rolled his eyes. "They're not in the entertainment business, Richard. They're serious scholars."

Hyacinth St. Claire gave Mr. Darcy a kiss on the cheek. "I, for one, would love hearing Dr. Bascombe speak on his subject. It would be thrilling!"

Catherine felt an imp prompt her to say, "His opening lecture is a psychological analysis of the Brontë sisters."

"Ooo," the woman cooed, her eyes alight. "How terribly . . . kinky!"

Catherine shuddered. What had she let Harry in for?

The gossip laughed. Catherine was suddenly afraid he would feature them on his show in an unsavory light. "Dr. Bascombe is an expert on several other writers as well—Joseph Conrad, Thomas Hardy, George Eliot. I assure you he is a respected authority at Oxford."

Mr. Darcy sat up, and Catherine thought he looked exactly like a hound who had caught the scent of the fox. "Oxford? You are from Oxford?"

Harry looked amused. "Of course, didn't we say?"

"No. You failed to mention it. I say, I believe you are going to be a tremendous hit! Give me details."

Catherine cut in, "The details haven't been decided."

Harry gave her a grateful look, Darling, how's the ankle?"

"It's throbbing rather. I'm afraid it needs some ice."

"We'll say our goodnights, then."

They both stood. Harry said, "Thank you for inviting us tonight, but we both have seminars in the morning, so I think it's best if we leave."

"I'm anxious for you to investigate this matter," said Danforth. "Westerman says Daphne will be out tomorrow on bail. Perhaps you could come by my house in the evening and talk to her. I'm not going to hear of her going home alone to her house in that murderous district where she lives. I can send my driver to pick you up in Westwood. You're at the inn?"

"Yes," said Catherine. She turned to Harry, "Is that all right, darling?"

"Topping," he said. "What time?"

"After dinner. Eightish?"

They settled the details, and Catherine and Harry made their way out of the club after assuring everyone that it had been a delight to meet them. Catherine remembered to limp.

"Sorry if I got you into hot water there," she apologized.

"That Darcy is a menace, and he's no more British than I am Chinese," Harry said.

"I'm afraid he's going to be going around Hollywood claiming you are his greatest friend."

"Heaven help me," Harry said.

As they drove back to Westwood, Harry asked, "Well, what did you think? Did we learn anything?"

"Joe Calloway is a flagrant anti-Semite and disliked Daphne on the strength of it," said Catherine. "It was rather difficult to listen to, actually. That's why I faked a sprain. He said this was a Jew town. What do you suppose he meant by that?"

"No idea. Sickening for you. Sorry."

"Did you have any luck with the divine Hyacinth?"

"She was trying to vamp me. But I gathered from a bit here

and there that she was a woman scorned. Michael Fields preferred Daphne to her, and it rather stung."

"Hmm. Daphne doesn't seem to be popular."

"Except with Buck. He worships her, I think. Unless it's all an act. You never know where you are with actors."

Chapter Six

Catherine's Tuesday seminar was, as it turned out, very much like a tutorial. She had six female students and two weedy-looking young men, all ready to begin their fourth year. Her first class was on the early Twentieth Century authors John Galsworthy and E.M. Forster. Comparing them to the Victorian writers, she said that literature in her country didn't really change much until the Great War, which was the natural dividing line between Victorian and Modern Literature.

It proved challenging to get any responses to her questions from the group. The Great War did not seem to be of any particular interest to the scholars. Catherine was forced to admit that it meant very much less to Americans in terms of history than it did to the British. She had never realized that this national difference would so affect her seminar. She assigned them to read *Room with a View* and *A Man of Property* and write a 250-word essay comparing and contrasting the two writers.

The students silently left the room. Discouraged, Catherine hoped Harry had had better luck with his group than she had with hers. She didn't know if she had the right instincts to understand American students.

Harry met her for lunch in the Faculty Dining room, which

was almost deserted as few students were taking the shortened summer term.

"I wonder if Daphne Binoche has had her arraignment yet. I do hope Mr. Danforth is planning on giving her some time with her father before he whisks her away to his house," she said to Harry. "How did your seminar go?"

"Not too well. Mostly women. I think they were a bit afraid of me."

"Probably in awe. You *do* look like a film star, you know. Too bad your Doppelgänger, Douglas Fairbanks, Jr., is filming in Britain right now! It might be fun for you to meet him."

He laughed. "You've been in Los Angeles too long. How was your class?"

"Pretty subdued. I think my students were shocked I gave them so much reading. I didn't seem to connect."

"Yes. They are very different from Oxford students. I got the feeling that they are not used to being asked their opinions," said Harry.

After lunch, they drove back to Westwood Village and walked down its streets for an hour in the mid-afternoon heat. The stores were new and different from the typical British village stores. A couple of art galleries graced the street near to where the inn stood. The art was all very modern and bold. Another road had a small health spa. Next to the door, a sign informed them that they could get a massage, a facial, a Swedish sauna, hair tints, cuts, and manicures.

They also discovered an ice cream "parlor," which they gratefully entered to escape the heat. Catherine had a dish of strawberry ice cream, while Harry chose a sundae with chocolate fudge syrup.

Refreshed by their treats, they walked back to the inn. They collapsed in front of the fans in the lounge. Harry had the desk ring the professor's room, but there was no answer. Catherine took this to be good news. She had brought a copy of *Room With a View* with her from Oxford, so she spent the late afternoon re-reading while Harry worked crosswords in a book he'd bought aboard ship.

* * *

What did Californians wear in the evenings when they were at home? Catherine wondered as she pondered her limited wardrobe after dinner. She decided she couldn't go wrong with her little black dress. It was midcalf with lattice trim on the bodice.

She met Harry downstairs just as the Danforth chauffeur came to call for them. Buck Danforth's car was a long-hooded fashionable Rolls Royce. They climbed in and seated themselves in the luxurious back seat, and the chauffeur showed them a pull-down bar where they might help themselves to a drink.

Both Harry and Catherine declined, preferring to watch the scenery as they drove further west. Eventually, they saw a neon-lit sign advertising the Beverly Wilshire Hotel.

Ah, now we get to see where the wealthy people live.

Since it wasn't yet dark, they could see Beverly Hills' mansions, set back from the street. She was a bit surprised. They were primarily replicas of some era of English architecture—Tudor, Norman, Georgian, even Gothic. Some appeared to be as large as small castles.

They knew they had arrived at the right place by the crowd of reporters outside the locked gates. They shouted questions: "Are you here to see Miss Binoche? Is she still under arrest? Who paid her bail? Who are you? What are you doing here?"

The chauffeur drove them expertly through the crowd, and the gates closed behind them. The Danforth mansion was Georgian, built of red brick with black shutters and white trim. The chauffeur stopped the car along the circular driveway at the front entrance. They thanked him, and the door was answered almost immediately by a stately butler. He took them through the black and white tiled hall to the drawing room, where Danforth and Miss Binoche were seated holding brandy snifters. The professor was there, as well, and they could smell the peppermint of his Schnapps. Buck and Dr. Adler rose at once.

They all shook hands, and Buck inquired about what they would have to drink.

Catherine asked for tonic water and Harry a whiskey. Going to the bar, Buck prepared the libations. Catherine and Harry sat down on an overstuffed white sofa across from Daphne Binoche. Catherine was relieved to see that the woman now looked more tranquil in a filmy lavender creation far more suited to her than the canvas prison uniform. Lincoln Fields' jail would have been an ordeal for anyone.

The professor said, "Dr. Bascombe, you haven't met my daughter, Dafna . . . rather Daphne Binoche as she calls herself these days. Daphne, this is Dr. Bascombe. He is also here to teach in the summer program."

Miss Binoche said, "I appreciate all the help on offer." The color of her gauzy evening gown brought out the color of her very expressive lavender eyes.

"What can you tell us about Michael Fields? What could have led to his murder?" asked Catherine.

Miss Binoche tossed her head so her long wavy hair was no longer covering one eye. "Michael was a complex man, as brilliant people often are. I don't think I can sum him up for you in a few words."

"Yesterday, you said you suspected his wife of killing him," Harry said. "Did they have a difficult marriage?"

"More than difficult. Absolutely fraught. Michael was always saying he was going to divorce her, but he never did. I could never understand that."

"He was Catholic," said Buck simply.

"In an age where people are shucking their religious principles right and left, that doesn't seem like a good enough reason," said Miss Binoche.

Buck shrugged. "It's a fact."

Professor Adler spoke up, "I have Catholics as patients. Their fear of damnation is very deeply felt. In Vienna, Catholics never divorce. They have multiple extramarital affairs, but they never divorce."

"Tell us about the marriage," Catherine said.

Daphne shrugged in the French manner. "Michael would have been a difficult man to be married to. I can't deceive myself. If I hadn't been such friends with Buck, I might have been taken in by him," she said. "I had the feeling there was always another woman in his life. Just lately, I suspected it was the ingenue."

"Miss St. Claire?" asked Harry.

Catherine remembered what he had said about Hyacinth and found it very unlikely that such a successful and complex man would harbor a passion for such an obvious trollop.

Daphne apparently read her doubt. She said, "Yes. I failed to see the attraction, but she is an ambitious little chit. She wants my job, frankly."

"Now, darling," said Buck. "You know that will never happen. You have a contract, for one thing. For another, the girl can't act her way out of a paper bag."

"Tell us about Mr. Fields's wife and family," requested Harry.

"His wife goes by her maiden name—Ruth Delano. I gather she's some kind of distant relative of the President. The family has been in New York as long as the Roosevelt's, and I learned from Buck that that's a long time by American standards. She's a terrific bore. A stage actress on Broadway. She has an apartment on Manhattan and lives there most of the time."

"Was she here at the time of the murder?"

Daphne rolled her eyes. "Oh, yes. Someone had told her that I was Michael's latest fling, and she came here to see for herself. She was tremendously offensive to me. Called me a 'wretched little Jewess.'"

There was definitely something studied about the actress's performance. It didn't ring true. Her shoulders had slumped, and she put a hand to her head. "I'm suddenly exhausted, Buck. I want to go upstairs." Turning to Harry and Catherine, she said, "Thank you for coming, but I don't think anyone can get me out of this mess."

Telling them he would return shortly, Buck helped the woman up from the sofa, and, arm around her waist, he led her upstairs. Catherine didn't doubt her exhaustion. Who could have slept in that awful jail? But why had she suddenly become nervous about talking?

The professor stood, sighing. "I must go to her. This has damaged her spirit. She's isn't my Dafna. It is very bad."

She envied Miss Binoche her father, at that moment. Catherine was in the process of mending her relationship with her father, but he would never be what one would call nurturing.

She raised her brows at Harry. Should they go?

"I think we need to stay and talk to Buck," he said, reading her mind. "He can tell us more than we have right now, which isn't much."

When Buck returned, he seemed preoccupied, which was understandable. Harry tried prompting him, "I understand the Fields have children?"

Danforth tossed his head slightly and brought himself to the moment. He paced the rug, hands in his pockets. "A Del and Alvira. They're both at UCLA. Ruth wanted them to go to better schools back East, but neither wanted to leave California." He paused to light a cigarette with the heavy chrome lighter on the mantel. "The daughter lives at home. Del lives on campus. I know very little about either of them. However, I do know that Michael was somewhat of a controlling father." After a moment, he added, "Oh, and Alvira wants to be an actress. I think she has an actor boyfriend Michael disapproved of. Anyway, that's the gist. I don't have particulars."

"I know it is an obvious question, but we have to start somewhere: Is there anyone on the set that would have ill feelings toward Mr. Fields?" asked Catherine.

"I'm not aware of anyone, but we all play our cards pretty close to our vests with a vulture-like Darcy haunting the set."

"I can't even imagine a woman carrying a gun," she said. "Did everyone know Miss Binoche had one?" asked Catherine.

"They all did. She made a joke of it. Like I said, I bought it for her because of her dangerous neighborhood. She carried it to please me."

They spoke a while longer, but Buck was unwilling to talk specifics. She wondered if Harry, too, sensed that he and the actress were holding things back. Beginning to doubt the actors' enthusiasm for the Professor's intervention in the form of two British sleuths, Catherine decided they weren't going to learn anything further tonight. She stood.

"Well, I can see that you're worried about Miss Binoche. We'll leave so you can return to her."

Buck released a pent-up breath. "Thank you so much for coming," he said. "I'm not sure we were able to tell you much. Daphne is knackered."

The word set off alarms in Catherine's head. "Knackered" was colloquially British. But maybe Americans used it, too?

"You have a lovely home," she said. "It almost seems as though we're back in England. Don't worry. We can call a cab to get us back to Westwood."

"Wouldn't think of it," said Buck. "There is a gaggle of reporters out there. Owens will drive you." He pulled a rope suspended in the corner of the room, and the butler appeared.

"Tell Owens he's needed to drive these folks back now," Buck instructed his minion.

* * *

"Well, that wasn't terrifically fruitful," said Catherine when they had negotiated the noisy crowd who photographed them through the car windows. Harry didn't reply until Owens dropped them off at the Inn.

"I don't know why Buck wanted us to come," said Harry, walking into the lounge.

"Both of them were quite obviously acting. But the professor seems genuinely alarmed. I feel that he, at least, knows his daughter well."

Harry said, "How do you get an actor not to act? I mean, I expect many people try to act in circumstances such as these. It's just that actors are so good at it. How do you get to the truth in cases like this?"

They were sitting in the lounge. The bar was open, and Harry ordered a whiskey for himself and tonic water for Catherine.

She said, "I have no idea. But I suppose one has to cultivate a relationship of trust. They're acting because they are trying to cover up at least part of the truth. Miss Binoche could be keeping back something quite harmless, but it could as likely be a big secret that would give her a motive for the murder."

"Despite our professor's feelings, I somehow am having a hard time believing in her innocence," said Harry, taking a sip of his drink and gazing thoughtfully in its depths. "She was certainly leading us up the garden path about Hyacinth and Fields."

"I agree. Like you, I wonder why Buck asked us over this evening," Catherine mused.

Harry said, "He invited us before Miss Binoche had even been arraigned. He obviously didn't realize she had no intention of talking."

"That's odd, I think," said Catherine taking her bottom lip between her teeth and worrying it. "Don't you think he'd know about something like that?"

"Perhaps he's finding out he doesn't know her as well as he thinks he does."

Catherine got up and strolled to the window. "Harry, everything is so different here. I was sort of prepared for New York. But all this seems . . . well, foreign."

"It is different. But aside from our lackluster students, we have seen only a slice of the population. Film stars, I imagine, live in their own world. It may or may not be entirely real. At least real in our sense. We've been to a jail, an exclusive nightclub, a Beverly

Hills mansion. We each have a class of unresponsive youngsters and have partaken of new experiences in cuisine—'meatloaf.' Ugh. In the absence of a good pub, perhaps we should embrace the unfamiliar tomorrow have a go at the beach. It's not far away."

"That sounds heavenly," said Catherine. "Unless we hear from the professor again, I think we've been dismissed from the case. And I don't have another seminar for a day. Are you prepared?"

"Darling, I could teach this subject in my sleep."

CHAPTER SEVEN

Morning found Catherine still sleeping in the cool breeze from her open window. Harry woke her with a knock on the door.

When she answered, she saw that he was fully dressed in his professor clothes.

"No beach?" she asked with a frown.

"Maybe later. The professor called. Daphne has gone missing--in violation of her bail agreement. If he finds out, Louis Mayer may start spitting nails."

"So, what are we supposed to do about it?" Catherine asked.

"Dr. Adler wants to talk to us. He's worried she might harm herself. I think he just needs someone to talk to who is outside this whole thing."

"Is he here at the inn?"

"No. He stayed with Buck Danforth last night. That's where Daphne was supposed to be."

"All right. Just give me time to resurrect myself. I'll meet you in the lobby."

* * *

The butler, Ames, greeted them at the Danforth residence and showed them into a yellow-painted morning room where the professor awaited them. His face was white with dark smudges under his eyes.

"Buck just left," he said. "He already searched her house. Now he is going to search the beaches. That is where she liked to go."

Catherine had been thinking. "I expect she wanted to go somewhere people wouldn't bother her. There's a man who has a radio show who spews gossip. And the press has been hounding her."

"But why wouldn't she talk to *me*?" he asked. "She knows I don't think she's guilty."

"Sometimes, a woman just has to be alone," Catherine said gently. "Does she have any particular friends? Women friends?" "She never spoke of any. She was not the sort of person who had women friends. Buck is the only friend she ever wrote about."

"Well, Dr. Adler, I don't think at this juncture that there is any reason to think something bad has happened to her," Harry said.

Catherine was silently cursing the woman for not having left a note. She must have known her father would worry about her. Not to mention Buck.

Catherine recalled the impression she had had the night before. "Did she say anything to you last night when you went up to her? Did she seem like herself?"

He shook his head slowly. "She was not the sweet Dafna I know. She put on an act for me. I have horrible suspicions." His eyes clouded with worry.

Harry went to him, where he stood by the window looking out with his back to them. He put a hand on the professor's shoulder. "How about telling us what you are afraid of? There's a good fellow."

Dr. Adler's voice was low and scratchy when it came. "She is changed. And it is a change clear through. Like she has been through . . . *das Erdbeben*."

Catherine looked at Harry for a translation. He said, "An earthquake?"

"Yes," said the professor. "Everything she used to wear on the surface. Now, it is not. It is all down deep. I, her father, do not know her anymore." He paused and grimaced. "These feelings you see now—she makes them bigger . . ."

"Exaggerates?" suggested Catherine.

"She exaggerates them, but they are not her feelings," Adler said.

"She is acting?" asked Harry. "How long has it been since you have seen your daughter?"

The professor said, "Last time was a year ago, no longer. When she was in Paris. It was Hanukkah. I have not seen her since she decided to come to America."

"And why did she decide to come to Hollywood, do you know?" asked Catherine.

"The big man. The director. He went to Paris to find her. He had seen her on the Cinema in America. He spent a week in Paris, and finally, she said, yes, she would go to Hollywood."

Harry and Catherine exchanged a look. It sounded suspiciously like Fields's tactics had involved a lot of wining and dining and perhaps something even more intimate.

"It is not a small thing to be a movie star in America," the professor said. "But I am afraid of the damage it has done to my daughter's psyche."

"Perhaps she will decide to go back to Paris now," said Harry, patting the old man on the shoulder.

"That would be my hope."

Catherine suddenly had an unpleasant suspicion. She thought of the cocaine culture she had encountered in the jazz scene in England. All that extravagant behavior—was it possible Miss Binoche was taking drugs? Had she gone somewhere and deliberately taken an overdose? Catherine shuddered. Harry, who was always attuned to her feelings, looked at her with a question in his eyes. She gave a minute shake of her head.

The professor said, "I wish we would hear from Mr. Danforth."

Catherine knew she needed to distract him. "Why don't you sit down and tell us more about your family?" she invited.

Taking a long breath, Dr. Adler did as she asked. Daphne's

mother wasn't Jewish but a Russian beauty who had lost her mother early. She had initially come to Vienna with her father, the diplomat. He had gone back to Russia, but his daughter had fallen in love with Vienna and stayed there, attending the University of Vienna as one of their few female students. Tatiana, as she was called, had taken all of the professor's classes and showed great promise as a psychologist.

For a reason Dr. Gerhardt Adler had never understood, the straightforward woman had fallen in love with him. One look into her lavender eyes, and he was smitten before he knew where he was. With no parents to stand in their way, they had married and been very happy until she had died of influenza when Daphne was a teenager. His daughter had become his life and his consolation. "Sometimes, when I look at her, she is her mother."

Buck Danforth returned from scouring the beaches by lunchtime. His eyes looked like they had burned through their sockets.

"I'm worried," he said. "There is something I think you should know, Professor, though I hate to add to your concerns." Sitting down, Buck shaded his eyes with his hand and sighed deeply. Then, seeming to come to a resolution, he withdrew his hand and leaned forward in his chair.

"Daphne is being stalked like a wild animal. I'm sure you would call her stalker a psychotic. She has even received death threats. I'm just praying her disappearance doesn't have to do with either of those things. Until now, I thought that Ruth Fields was behind the threats, " said Buck. "But I don't think she would kidnap Daphne. If she has been taken, there's a man behind this."

Catherine looked at the professor. He was clearly stunned, and she thought he couldn't have had worse news. Unless Daphne was dead. "These threats," he said, his voice trembling. "What did they say?"

Buck looked even wearier if that were possible. Taking a large wallet from his jacket pocket, he drew out a piece of paper and handed it to the man. "That is one of the letters. They all came by post."

The professor scanned it, giving a little cry. When he looked up, his eyes were dilated with fear. He passed the note to Catherine.

It was written on cheap paper. The threat had been typed: *The Germans have the right idea—you dirty little Jew Communist. You may have a fatal "accident" soon.*

Catherine passed the letter to Harry with hands that shook. "How perfectly dreadful! Were they all like that?"

"All the letters were some variation of this one," said Buck.

He walked to the French doors and looked out as though he were checking for someone hiding in his garden. "The notes started coming a couple of months ago. At first, she didn't take them to heart. Actors and actresses get all sorts of mail, from love letters to death threats. But then the stalking started, and she had a few accidents that could have been a lot worse than they were." Buck's hands fisted. "I feel so helpless!"

"What accidents?" asked the professor, his voice thin with strain.

Buck turned round to face them again. "The brakes went on her car. It could have been much worse, but she only crashed into a fence. She wasn't going fast. All that happened was that she got a nasty lump on the head."

"That could have killed her!" Catherine said. "How did they get at her car?"

"I've told you, she lives in an unsavory area where they have the old Mission-style architecture she likes. She parks on the street. All someone needed was a flashlight and a pair of wire cutters to cut the brake cables. It could have been done at night. No one in her neighborhood would have thought anything of it."

Gooseflesh covered Catherine's arms. She rubbed them with her hands. Her heart raced. "What do the police think?"

The professor's eyes were huge with alarm.

Buck said, "She wouldn't go to the police. Growing up in Austria, she feared them. I couldn't talk sense into her."

"What else happened?" Harry asked.

"He or she mixed poison with her face cream in her studio

dressing room. Fortunately, it smelled odd enough that she noticed it right away and sent for her make-up artist. She said she had not changed her creams. They had the new one analyzed, and it contained arsenic."

"Heavens!" said Catherine.

"Then, when Michael was killed, someone called in an anonymous tip to the police saying that they had heard Daphne and Michael arguing and she had threatened his life. That's one of the reasons they arrested her, I've always thought."

"It's worse than unfortunate that she didn't go to the police about the first two incidents," said Harry. "Now that she's a suspect in the murder, they probably won't believe her."

"Tell me about these 'stalkings,'" said the professor.

Catherine couldn't stay seated. She got up and started prowling across the Aubusson carpet.

Buck answered while lighting a cigarette at the mantel. "Hang-ups when she answers the telephone. She's often followed by the same black Ford when she drives to work and when she drives home. On those occasions, she doesn't get out of the car but comes over here and sounds her horn. I go out and escort her from her car to mine, then I take her where she's going. No one follows us when I get involved."

"Did you see anyone?" asked Harry.

"A big man in sunglasses and a Fedora. But he could have been someone who was hired to harass her."

Catherine rubbed her arms again. "She must be terrified. I'm surprised she didn't enlist the help of Louis Mayer."

"Until the brake lines were cut, she just thought it was a crazed fan," said Buck. "But I think it's some kind of war of nerves this fellow is playing."

"To what end?" asked Harry.

"Who knows?" said Buck. "He's a sick blighter."

The professor was silent, and his cheeks were wet with tears. Catherine realized that something like this was just what he had feared. She wanted to take his hands and comfort him, but she hesitated to take such liberties with a man she scarcely knew.

She said, "I can't even imagine how you must feel . . ."

The butler coughed slightly and entered. "There is a young lady here for Miss Binoche. She said she was told to come here. I don't like to tell her anything in case she is with the press."

Catherine marveled at the man's discretion. He had been trained well.

"Did she give you a card?" Buck asked.

The butler handed it to him.

"Who is Lady Naomi Wadsworth?" Buck asked as though speaking to himself.

"Lady Naomi!" repeated Catherine. She threw a look at Harry, who didn't seem inclined to answer. "She came on our ship. Harry knows her. Didn't you say she is Miss Binoche's great friend, Harry?"

"Confound it!" said Harry. "Doesn't she read the papers? Doesn't she realize this is not time for a social call? I will see her. Where did you put her, Ames?"

"In the drawing room," the butler said.

"Catherine, please feel free to come with me." Harry's brow was furrowed in annoyance, and he was slightly flushed.

Lady Naomi was walking about the room, perfectly assembled as always, examining the indifferent pictures. "Harry? But what are *you* doing here? Where is Daphne? Don't tell me I've come to the wrong house!"

"She's staying here, but I'm afraid she's out at the moment," said Harry. "This is my colleague, Miss Tregowyn." Pausing, he slid an arm around Catherine's waist. "Darling, this is Lady Naomi Wadsworth."

The visitor looked Catherine over, a brow raised. Catherine put out a hand. "How do you do?"

"Well enough, thank you," the woman said, offering Catherine two fingers. "Do you two know Daphne?"

"We are just here visiting Miss Binoche's father. Professor Adler. We met him on the Queen Mary."

"*He* is her father?" Now both her elegant eyebrows were raised.

"Yes," said Harry. "He is here from Vienna, visiting her. How did you know to come here and not Miss Binoche's house?"

"Not that it's any business of yours, but she left a message for me at the Beverly Wilshire where I'm staying."

"When?" asked Catherine. "When did she leave the note?"

Lady Naomi looked at her hard as though wondering by what right she asked the question. "At two this morning, as a matter of fact. Whose house is this?"

Catherine felt tremendous relief. Surely Daphne must have been out and about on her own if she left a note for her friend at two a.m.

Harry answered, "It belongs to a friend of hers. I can't say when she'll be back. Shall I have her ring you?"

"Is this Fields' house? You might as well tell me," the visitor said.

"No. I guess you wouldn't know, what with being in the Grand Canyon, but Mr. Fields has been murdered."

Lady Naomi's eyes widened. "Really!" While she absorbed the shock, she began removing her gloves. "Well, that's torn it. I've come all this way for nothing, as it turns out. Daphne had arranged a screen test for me."

The woman's self-absorption clearly knew no bounds. What was Harry going to do with her?

"Well, this isn't the best time to visit, Nay," said Harry, his face hard. "If you listened to the news, you would know that Miss Binoche is out of jail on bail for the murder. I think she will have other things on her mind than your screen test."

"Oh!" The woman was utterly taken aback, and for a moment, her face was blank with shock. Then she seemed to recover and pulled off the other glove. "Well, you don't have to be so nasty,

Harry. She's my good friend. Of course, she will want to see me. I can offer to help."

Before Harry could object, Lady Naomi moved past him, headed for the drawing room.

Harry rolled his eyes, imploring the heavens. Catherine stifled a laugh. "You are going to have to tell me about your past with this woman someday," she said. "At least she brought good news. Miss Binoche was alive at 2:00 a.m."

"Confound it! She needs to go away," said Harry, his eyes narrowed in anger.

* * *

Lady Naomi charmed the professor, but Buck stood apart from his guests, maintaining a grim exterior. Catherine couldn't believe that Lady Naomi could consider herself welcome under the circumstances and didn't blame Buck for his murderous glances.

Ames announced luncheon.

"Lay an extra place," Buck said shortly.

During luncheon, Lady Naomi regaled them with tales of flying over the Grand Canyon. No one even appeared to be listening to her, but she spoke on.

Irritation played along Catherine's nerves. *She has the most colossal opinion of herself. Couldn't she see that she was not wanted? She acts for all the world as though she is granting us a favor by being here. And what is Daphne playing at, running about in the middle of the night? Was she the victim of foul play? If not, how could she worry her father so?*

Ames came into the room. "The press have breached the fence, sir. Would you like to make a statement?"

Rather than being annoyed, Buck was thoughtful, "I wouldn't be surprised if they've had someone watching overnight. Maybe they saw her leave and followed her. It could be that in this case, they know more than we do."

"You know, you could be right," said Harry. "I'll go see if I can find anything out without giving anything away, shall I?"

Buck nodded.

He left the room, and soon they heard the front door close. Catherine cranked the casement window open slightly above the buffet so they could listen to what was going on.

Before Harry could even introduce himself, they were asking, "Who was Daphne meeting at 2:00 in the morning? What was she doing at the Beverly Wilshire?"

"Seems to me that you know an awful lot more than I do," said Harry. "I just got here and have been waiting for her return."

"Who are you?" asked a woman in black trousers.

"I'm an old friend. I'm here with my wife, actually, but I know you lot and how you like to make things up, so I've no further comment. Was she at the Beverley Wilshire? How the devil do you know that?"

"The doorman gave us a call. He's friendly."

"Meaning he's in your pay?"

"You got it. I don't want you to think we don't show our appreciation."

"Well, I don't know anything, so save your appreciation for someone who does. We're in the dark concerning Miss Binoche."

"We'll be hanging around in case you remember anything, Lord Posh."

"You'd best do your hanging around on the opposite side of the gate, or Mr. Danforth will ring the police!"

As they were moving off, a man cried, "Lord Posh!" Harry turned his head. A flash went off. Harry only hoped he didn't have his mouth open.

* * *

By the time they had finished eating the interminable meal, it was 2 p.m. At last, Catherine could hear the telephone ringing in the butler's pantry. Ames called Mr. Danforth to the telephone. "It's

Miss Binoche, sir," he said, showing a very slight edge of eagerness.

They had adjourned to the drawing room, and Catherine was finding it increasingly difficult not to strangle Lady Naomi. She talked about her trip to Monte Carlo in July and how dreadfully hot it had been, but "nothing to what it is here!"

Buck returned finally. Catherine was glad to see that his face was relaxed, and there was a new light in his eyes.

"That was Daph. I have to go collect her in Malibu."

She watched as Professor Adler sagged with relief. "She is all right?" he asked.

"She sends multiple apologies for the scare she has given all of us. It seems she walked on the beach for hours thinking. She then found a crummy little beach hotel and went to sleep for longer than she intended. She just woke up. You'll be happy to know, Professor, she sounded like the old Daphne. And she wants Catherine and Harry to stay. She asked for them particularly."

"But I feel like we're intruding," said Catherine.

"She has something, in particular, she wants to tell you," Buck said.

Chapter Eight

Though Daphne's face was scoured entirely of makeup, her hair in a frizzy cloud, and her skirt and shawl embedded with beach sand, she was still beautiful.

She immediately took charge. The difference in her voice and demeanor was startling. To Catherine, it seemed as though she had suddenly awakened from a refreshing sleep. She was a woman in charge.

"Oh, Naomi, good. You're here. Papa, my love, can you ever forgive me? I needed to think. You know, I always do my best thinking when I am walking, and I have come to love the ocean."

She turned her smile on Catherine and Harry. "I'm so sorry to inconvenience you. You were so good to come to my father's aid. Can I ask for a further indulgence? Can you stay for just a little longer?

"I should like to talk to you, specifically. But I am getting sand all over. I must take a quick bath. Naomi, darling, come with me. We can talk."

Everyone spoke at once, reassuring her.

She dashed up the stairs, Naomi following obediently, while the rest of them stood in the hall, watching her. Then they broke into speech, saying how well she looked.

Catherine suspected that more than one of them had feared she might never be seen again alive. And here she was, radiant with purpose. This was not the woman Catherine had seen at the jail, nor yet the one she had seen last night. She was very anxious to learn more about her, especially in light of all the professor's fond memories.

* * *

Fortunately, for everyone's peace of mind, Daphne first had apparently reassured Lady Naomi about her concerns. After about ten minutes, the lady came trailing down the stairs smiling at all of them.

"Harry, darling, could you walk me to my car? I don't feel I can brave the press alone," Lady Naomi said.

It was a transparent ruse, and Catherine was annoyed. Through the still-open window, she heard the press greet Harry.

"Lord Posh! Who is this lovely lady?"

"Lady Naomi Wadsworth," Harry replied. "Surely you have heard of her?"

Catherine smiled to herself.

"Should we have?" one reporter asked.

"She is terribly well-known in Britain. She has lately been making solo flights over the Grand Canyon. Perhaps she will tell you about it!"

Then while the press were besieging the woman, he quietly moved away toward the house.

"Lady Naomi, are you a friend of Daphne Binoche? What can you tell us about her? Can you give us a statement? What is your relationship to Lord Posh?" Catherine laughed as she heard. She was sure Lady Naomi was thrilled to once again be the center of attention.

"How ever did you get past the press with Daphne in the car?" Harry asked Buck Danforth once he was back in the drawing room.

"You saw her! She was completely unrecognizable. We sailed right through the gate," said their host.

"And she really is all right?" asked the professor again.

"Better than all right. Daphne says she has finally settled things in her mind, and she is ready to talk," said Buck.

The professor looked stricken. "What is she going to tell us? She didn't commit that murder!"

Catherine had had the same thought. There had been something fey about Daphne Binoche as she came through that door. She had seemed not entirely of this earth.

* * *

All of them—Daphne's father, Daphne, Buck Danforth, Harry, and Catherine—were seated in the drawing room. It was hot with the sun coming in from the French doors out onto the terrace. They each held a glass of cold lemonade.

"What I have to say should never leave this room," said Daphne. "It is intensely private, and I have never spoken of it to anyone. I don't want the press to get hold of it, and it could strengthen the police's case against me. Catherine and Harry, I am trusting you with this because my father trusts you to help me, and since I don't know what else to do, I am trusting you, too."

Both Catherine and Harry nodded. It felt to Catherine as though she had been drawn into a circle of sacred trust. Without knowing what Daphne Binoche was about to say, she could only hope she would never be required to break that trust.

The woman stood up. She was now dressed in a fitted black dress which came to mid-calf and flared at the knees. There was a long rope of pearls about her neck, and her lipstick was red. She made an exotic, stunning figure.

Going to the mantel, she put her hand upon it and rested it there. "I have never been in love before, but I loved Michael Fields from the bottom of my soul." She paused to let this sink in.

The revelation did not surprise Catherine, but she looked at Buck. His face went ashen.

"I had no thoughts of ever coming to Hollywood," she continued. "I was very happy in Paris. But in the space of one week, all that changed." Bringing her hand up to the back of her neck, she rubbed it as though she could remove the tension. "I remember the exact moment. We stood on Pont Neuf, overlooking the Seine."

Catherine could see that she was steeped in the past, viewing the distant scene.

"His eyes were the same gray as the sky that day. He looked straight into me, and we connected soul to soul. It was more a spiritual connection than a physical one.

"I wanted to know everything about him. We talked as we walked Paris for days. We held hands. It was all so innocent. Then he told me that he was married."

Here she stopped, taking a handkerchief from her pocket and wiping her eyes.

"I was devastated. I had seen firsthand what relationships looked like when one partner was married. To add to my pain, he told me he didn't believe in divorce."

"I was furious. I felt Michael had led me on." She paused, taking in a little gasp of air that turned into a sob. For a moment, she couldn't go on. Then she said, "He admitted he had but didn't think his marriage would be a stumbling block considering what we felt for one another. I told him I couldn't have such a relationship. It was against all my principles."

"But, *Schatzi*, whyever did you come to Hollywood after that?" asked her father.

"I couldn't stay away. I had to be with Michael. But our affair was only emotional. I would never let it go further. Now . . . well, now . . . I am torn apart. Part of my world has ended. I left last night because I needed to grieve, but I didn't want anyone to see." Her tears were falling freely now, and she sniffed. Catherine wondered how she managed to look so appealing when she cried.

Buck stood slowly like a very old man. He walked out of the room like one blind. Daphne hardly seemed to notice; she was so caught up in her performance. Catherine wondered how this could be news to him. Surely he had guessed! And if he had, the situation gave him a powerful motive.

"The only thing I live for now is to find out who did this horrible thing," said Daphne, staring at the door through which Buck had retreated. "But I don't want anyone to know about Michael and me. The police would think I killed him in a fit of . . . of . . . rage because he wouldn't get a divorce."

Catherine spoke. "I am very sorry for the grief you must feel." Her words felt as insufficient as a drop of rain in a pool of water, but she went on. "You mentioned at the jail that you thought his wife had done it."

"Yes. I still do. She thought we were having an affair. Someone from the cast wrote or phoned her and told her. Ruth flew home from New York right away. Her relationship with Michael was complicated. I've never understood it."

"This is going to be difficult, Dafna," her father said gently. "We are Jewish."

"I know. I never forget that. I know how the cards are stacked against me. But I'm not going down. I'm going to figure out who did this. I'm not going to be the scapegoat."

"There are rumors about your relationship with Fields," said Catherine.

"Did you believe them?" Daphne asked.

"I didn't know what to think," confessed Catherine, feeling as though she were tied up in a sticky spider's web. Could she even believe Daphne Binoche? Was it possible amidst all Hollywood's drama to have such a restrained relationship as the actress described? Was her statement just a masterful job of acting? She wondered what Harry thought. And the professor. Did he believe his daughter? Catherine couldn't even imagine what Buck must be feeling. Daphne said, "If you will excuse me now. I must go to Buck. This has been a shock for him."

"We will say goodbye, then," Catherine said.

"Please wait," said Daphne. "I am certain there is more to discuss. Give me some time with dearest Buck, and then I will return."

When she had gone, and the door was closed behind her, Professor Adler threw up his hands. "I do not even know my own daughter anymore."

Harry said, "Herr Doktor, I'm sure this has been a shock to you. I know it has been to me. We'll be back in shortly, but Catherine is peaky. She needs some air. Come out on the terrace, darling. You're as white as a ghost."

Catherine hated to abandon the poor professor, but obviously, Harry needed to get something off his chest. As she walked by Dr. Adler, she put a hand on his shoulder. "Never mind. We shall be back in again soon."

She followed Harry out the French door onto the terrace, which overlooked a large lawn fringed by rose bushes oddly juxtaposed with the inevitable palms. It was jarring, just like Daphne's confession given before Buck was jarring.

"That was unnecessarily unkind," she said to Harry. "To Buck, I mean. He worships her."

"It was a performance," said Harry coldly. "The woman obviously thrives on making an exhibition of her emotions."

"She's very French, isn't she? Or perhaps Russian. Like her mother."

"I must say, I don't care for her much," said Harry. "French, Austrian, or Russian."

"Her emotions do run hot. I can't imagine her hiding them all this time."

"She obviously didn't," said Harry, narrowing his eyes against the sun. "Hence the rumors." He strolled to the edge of the terrace, then turned around and walked back. "What I wanted to tell you is that we could be trying to defend a murderess," said Harry. "Even her father says she's changed."

Daphne had obviously rubbed him the wrong way. The actress

had misread her audience. Catherine realized she wasn't entirely in sympathy with the woman, either. Sitting down on a lawn chair, she felt perspiration coming out all over in the unforgiving heat.

"What tack do you think we ought to take?" she asked.

"I have no idea. I guess we should find out the salient facts before we make a decision. I wouldn't want to let the old boy down. I can't imagine what we'll do if they find her guilty."

* * *

When the actress and Buck returned to the room, he seemed to have regained his composure. Catherine wondered what the woman could possibly have said that would have softened the blow she had dealt. Daphne had now adopted the appearance of a repentant sinner—head bowed hands clasped as she sat next to Buck on the sofa.

"You two are our only connection to all the people involved in this," Catherine said. "Could you give us some insight into the other members of the cast or anyone else who was close to Mr. Fields?"

Buck spoke up, a pucker between his well-marked brows. "It's actually not that big of a cast. You met Hyacinth St. Claire, the ingenue who is also the victim in the movie. She was making up to Michael—wanted Daphne's role. She is totally unsuited for it. But I don't see that she has a motive for killing Michael. Quite the opposite."

"Yes," said Harry. "That was my impression. While we were dancing, she had a go at Daphne and all the reasons she was unsuitable for the role. Hyacinth said that the only reason Daphne had gotten the role was that she was Fields's mistress."

"Michael was a brilliant director," said Buck. "He created my character. The playwright's conceptions were rather shallow. I don't know that our new director, Hale, has Michael's touch. It is certainly not in my best interests that he is dead."

Catherine discounted Buck's last statement. It was clear to

anyone with the least amount of sense that he was still head over ears for Daphne. How could he have helped but know of her passion for the director?

Catherine asked, "What can you tell me about John Hale?"

"He has some kind of in with Louis Mayer. I'm not sure what it is. I suspect he'll do an adequate job directing if he follows Michael's vision," said Daphne. "He possesses an ambitious wife and two young children. They were at the beach together when Michael was murdered."

Buck stroked her back. "Why don't you go upstairs and lie down?" he said. "You must be exhausted still. I can handle this."

Wordlessly and full of grace, the actress walked to the door of the room. Once there, she turned her head and said to Catherine and Harry, "I don't really know why you have agreed to help me. I hope you will continue to do so."

After she had departed, her father got up and followed her.

Buck said, "This is all terrible for her. She was there, you know."

"Yes," said Catherine. "She told me at the jail. They were at his apartment," she said.

"Michael lived in a service apartment when his wife was gone," Buck said. "He just wanted the simple life close to the studio with no servants fussing about. He had the house built for Ruth as a peace offering for dragging her across the country. But she has always abhorred Hollywood."

"I thought she had come back," said Catherine.

"Only just. Michael was delaying returning to live with her. She isn't an easy woman." Buck worried a hangnail on his right index finger. "Daphne thinks that Ruth Fields was the person at the door. He was shot point-blank in the hall. Daphne heard no conversation. The kitchen is at the back of the apartment."

Harry said, "Where was her pistol found?"

"On the floor next to Michael. Daphne heard the shot and rushed into the hall, but there was no one there. She didn't go after the killer; she tried to help Michael, but he was already dead. Shot right through the heart."

Catherine shuddered. "That must have been brutal for her. What did she do then?"

"I imagine she got a bit hysterical, but she finally thought to call the police. She never even noticed her gun, or I'm sorry to say, she would have removed it. It was distinctive—a pearl-handled affair. Definitely a woman's gun." The man began pacing. "And before you ask, yes. It was the gun that was used in the shooting. The bullet that killed him was fired from that gun. There is a way they can tell these days."

"But," said Harry. "How do they know it was *Daphne's* gun."

"Serial number. It shows I was the buyer, actually, but you know that I gave it to her."

A quick thought darted into Catherine's mind. *You could have stolen it back and used it to kill Michael Fields, framing Daphne.*

The same thought must have occurred to Harry, for he asked, "Did you know about Daphne and Fields?"

"I didn't know about it for certain until she told us today. But I had my suspicions she was just using me as a smokescreen."

Harry said, "Rough go, all the way around."

"It's been a brutal time for all of us," said Buck.

"Was Daphne carrying the gun because of the person who was following her?" asked Catherine.

"Yes. That's the only reason I gave it to her," said Buck.

Harry said, "That's rather important. Do the police know that? And what about the gun? Had she missed it? How did the murderer get hold of it?"

"The police don't know about the threats. And they simply refuse to believe that the gun had been missing for days. Personally, I think someone took it from Daphne's purse at the Starlight. It would have helped if she had reported the stalker to the police, not to mention the threats and the theft of her gun, but she didn't. She grew up frightened of the police. It's a rough go for the Jews in Vienna.

Catherine was of two minds about whether Buck had actually known of Daphne's connection to Michael Fields. Could Ruth Fields really be behind the death threats, the stalkings, and the murder? No. She was in New York. And the terrorizing sounded more like a man's game.

Buck ceased his pacing and rattled the change in his pocket. He was probably impatient for them to leave so he could go to Daphne.

"Thank you for sharing all of this," she said. "I only wish the police knew."

"She's under arrest for murder," Buck said. "They wouldn't take her seriously."

"Do they know she's a Communist?" asked Harry.

"Yes. They ran a check on Daphne with the Sûreté in Paris," said Buck.

"Surely they don't think Fields death was political?"

"The blighters are looking into every option. I'm sure her party affiliation isn't helping her situation."

She said, "We'll leave you now if you'll just give us Mrs. Fields' address. I'm sure we'll have lots more questions, of course, but you could use a break."

"I don't know the exact number of her house. But it's one street over from here. The only modern one on the block. It's white. Art Deco."

CHAPTER NINE

On the way to the Fields home, Catherine asked Harry, "What do you think about those 'accidents' and the stalking?"

"It sounds serious. I'd like to know who is behind it, obviously. But I doubt Daphne will be stalked as long as she's with Buck," Harry said.

"Good point," she said. "Look. That must be the Fields' house."

Catherine wasn't a fan of Art Deco exteriors. They were plain and white and made the buildings look like hospitals. Such was the case with the Fields' home. Catherine gave the butler their visiting cards and told him to tell his mistress they were there from the "studio" concerning her husband's death.

On their way up to the door, Harry and Catherine had decided on this strategy. It was the only thing they could think of. Catherine was not altogether happy with the lie, but she was anxious to see the woman and form an opinion.

The butler returned and told them Miss Delano would see them in the study. He took them through a pure white house—walls, floors, furniture. Framed black and white photo landscapes decorated the walls. The effect was cold and impersonal. Did the decorating reflect Fields' idea of his wife and marriage?

After all that, the study was a surprise. Catherine knew at once that it had belonged to the director. It had dark wood floors and paneling. The furniture was red leather. Behind a Queen Anne cherry desk sat a beautifully made-up blonde woman with shadowed eyes and hollow cheeks. She resembled a member of the English aristocracy.

When she spoke, she had an accent that was neither English nor American. It was halfway in between. "So MGM has sent you. I might have expected it of Louis. But I should think the culprit was obvious. She's only out on bail."

"There are a few things that don't add up," said Harry in a reasonable attempt at an American accent.

Catherine couldn't manage that, so she used her native Cornish accent, abandoning the Oxbridge language she customarily used. "You prefer your stage name, Miss Delano, I believe?"

"Yes, you're right. How may I help you?"

They had agreed that Harry would conduct the interview. "Do you have anyone who can verify your whereabouts at the time of the murder?"

She looked dumbfounded. "Surely you're not accusing me of my husband's murder!"

"We just think we ought to know what you told the police," Catherine rushed in to say.

"Well, I don't see how it can possibly matter to Louis, but I was watching my son play baseball that afternoon. He plays for UCLA."

Catherine had vaguely heard of baseball. It was some bastardized form of cricket.

"Did UCLA win the match?" Harry asked with a smile. "You must be very proud of him."

"Yes, to both. I am proud of Del. He gets his athleticism from me. I was a champion tennis player." She nodded to a portrait of herself in tennis whites on the bookshelf behind her.

"Do you believe that your husband was having an affair with Miss Binoche?"

"I'm altogether convinced. Though he denied it." She rolled

her dark blue eyes. "He insisted that they were just good friends. Have you ever heard any lie so pathetic?"

"She insists the same thing," said Harry. "Could it possibly be true?"

"I know a man in love. And I know my husband. Why do you think we live apart nine months out of the year? He occupied a position of power in Hollywood. He was also quite handsome in a Clark Gable sort of way. Women were constantly throwing themselves at him. I suspect this Jewess wasn't any different."

"How do you know she is Jewish?" Harry asked.

"I am well-informed. You've heard of Richard Darcy, of course? He makes it his business to find out these things."

Catherine's mind flew to the radio show host. Rather a weasel, she thought.

"Of course," Miss Delano continued, her voice and face complacent, "I can't really complain. I have my own lovers where I live in Manhattan. I had no reason to kill Mike. As a matter of fact, I am twice the actress Daphne Binoche is, but that is neither here nor there."

Catherine looked down at the Persian rug. Obviously, the widow was lying. Why else had she come racing home from New York when she found out her husband had a lover?

"Would it surprise you to know that someone is following Miss Binoche? And that her life had been attempted twice?"

Once again, the widow was speechless. She groped for the cigarette box and made an agitated job of lighting a cigarette.

"How alarming," she said finally. "Are you certain she's not manufacturing a drama to cover up her guilt?"

"Not unless you think she'd crawl under her car, cut the brake line, and then take the car out knowing she might kill herself," said Harry.

"Heavens!" Ruth Delano exclaimed. Taking a long drag on her cigarette, she sat back in her chair as though winded.

Catherine wondered if this was an outstanding example of the woman's acting.

"Do you know of anyone with a motive?" asked Harry.

"For cutting the brake line or killing my husband?"

"Both," he said, pinning her with his dark eyes. Harry could look dangerous when the occasion demanded it.

"Well, that little Hyacinth wanted the lead in the movie they're making. But I can't see her cutting brake lines. Maybe she hired it done." She shook her head as though she were trying to rid herself of the problem. Then she said, "As for my husband's murder—that friend of his. Buckingham Danforth. I suspect him of having a few dangerous secrets in his past. He doesn't ring true."

Catherine asked, "If the production should continue, do you think they will be able to find an actress of Miss Binoche's stature to replace her?"

Ruth Delano gave a self-satisfied smile. "Oh yes. It shouldn't be difficult at all. I'm available." She moved forward in her chair. "Now, I'm afraid I have an evening engagement. I must go begin the work of making myself presentable." She had clearly had much experience with having her wishes obeyed.

"Thank you for your time, Miss Delano. Is your daughter at home?" asked Harry.

"Unfortunately, no. She's out with that miserable boyfriend of hers. The would-be actor. Mike can't . . . couldn't stand him."

"And your son?"

"He lives in his own apartment. He studies at UCLA. As does my daughter, but she prefers the comforts of home. Of course, I wanted them both to go to the Ivy League, but they wanted to stay in California."

The woman stood, clearly expecting them to take their leave.

Catherine asked, "How did your children get along with your husband?"

"Now you suspect my children? They wouldn't even know how to fire a gun. They're complete innocents! My daughter is a Daddy's Girl, and Del is so completely concerned with his studies he never comes up for air."

Harry said, "Thank you again, Miss Delano. Have a pleasant evening."

As they walked down the hall to the front door, Catherine was shocked to see Joseph Calloway coming toward them. All three of them stopped dead.

"Mr. Calloway! What an unexpected surprise," she said. She noted that he carried a fresh gardenia corsage in a floral box. "How heavenly! A gardenia. I do adore gardenias!"

"Greetings!" said Calloway. "Yes. Ruth loves them as well. I thought I might come around to cheer her up. Her husband's death has been a rotten thing for her. An affair is bad enough, but having him killed by his mistress; well, that's not to be borne."

"So you believe Miss Binoche killed Michael Fields?" Harry asked. Meanwhile, Catherine's head was spinning. *Joe Calloway is courting the widow. Has he been in love with Ruth Fields all along? Does he have a motive?*

Chapter Ten

Catherine and Harry discussed the Calloway development all the way down the walkway to the car.

"He must have run of the house if the butler let him in when Mrs. Fields was getting ready for the evening," said Catherine.

"I wonder where they are going," said Harry. Why don't we park the car behind that hedge and see what happens? It seems to me it would be too early for dinner."

"Two minds with but the same thought," said Catherine. "I hadn't thought about it, but with Miss Binoche and Mr. Danforth gone, they must have called things off at the studio today,"

When he had started up the car, Harry said, "It will be interesting to see what happens now."

When the car was successfully parked behind the hedge, Catherine and Harry crept along the barrier to a small gap where they could see the Fields' house. They hoped the neighbors were otherwise occupied.

Catherine's watch made it half an hour before Calloway and Mrs. Fields exited the house. The woman was very animated and had her hand through Calloway's arm. She was a long way away from the vindictive, grieving widow they had visited.

Calloway's car was a Pierce-Arrow convertible, Harry told her as they sped away on its trail. The passengers in the sports car were oblivious to the fact that they were being followed.

"It looks like he's making his way to the beach," said Harry. "Maybe we'll get our afternoon there after all!"

"Darling, they're not dressed for swimming. I'm guessing they're on their way to Calloway's house," said Catherine, pulling out her sunglasses. "Whew, it's hot today!"

* * *

The drive was long, finally ending on an island that announced itself as "Balboa." It was surrounded by yachts. There was only one street of shops and restaurants. The rest of the island was covered in bungalows, except for the lots on the water. Those spots were built with huge mansions, and Joseph Calloway appeared to own one of them. It had its own garage. The pair were now quite lovey-dovey as they walked from the car to the three-story Mission-style house, which Calloway unlocked. In a surprise move, he scooped Ruth Fields up and carried her over the threshold. There was no doubt what was in store for the couple for the rest of the afternoon.

"Well, well, well," said Catherine. "Another man with a motive."

"I beg you will not so casually malign my sex. Ruth is fully capable of murder."

"So she is," said Catherine with a laugh. "Let's take a walk as long as we're here. I need the exercise."

The island proved delightful with an ice cream stand and a ferry boat which they road over to the Balboa Peninsula. There they found a lovely Mexican restaurant where they enjoyed an early dinner on the outdoor patio under an umbrella, which protected them from the sun.

"You know what I can't decide?" asked Catherine.

"What?"

"Who is the better actress: Daphne or Ruth?"

"I'm afraid the jury is still out," replied Harry.

"Maybe neither of them can resist acting out the role of a lifetime," said Catherine, sipping pink lemonade.

"Somewhere, I have heard that it takes a certain kind of chemistry to act in films. Not all stage actors can make the leap from stage to screen. Mrs. Fields may be one of them," said Harry. "That would have given her a definite animus against Daphne."

"And what about Buck?" he continued. "Or do you agree with Miss Delano that he's dangerous?"

"There's something off about him, but I can't put my finger on it," she said.

"He's definitely playing a role, and it's one we're familiar with. So familiar, I almost didn't see it," said Harry.

She agreed with Harry. "Yes! The English gentleman? You're right, darling. He also wasn't nearly as broken up about Daphne's confession of her love for Fields as I expected him to be."

"That was exceedingly odd," agreed Harry. "I'm not sure that wasn't the oddest thing about the whole day. He either worships her or is a better actor than I gave him credit for."

"So," said Catherine after placing her order. "You know, despite the American accent—I think he really is British. He used the word 'knackered,' and I remember it jolted me. But I do think the 'gentleman' is an act. The sort of gentleman he is acting out disappeared with the Edwardians."

"Well, the Edwardians haven't entirely disappeared, darling," said Harry. "Perhaps he was raised in Britain and aspired to be an Edwardian gentleman. Perhaps he was a servant." He paused and laughed. "It's rather tantalizing, isn't it? Buckingham Danforth, heartthrob of millions, in fact, a bootboy?" He wore a puckish grin.

When they made their way back to the car, Calloway's car was right where he'd left it.

* * *

After they arrived back at the inn, Harry had a nightcap while she tried to sum up their day.

In response to her fledgling theories, Harry said, "We simply don't know enough about these people to know what the truth is. With all of them acting out a charade, it's going to take some digging." He looked dimly at her tonic water.

"Darling, have you gone off liquor altogether? Won't you have a liqueur or something?"

"I have gone off. The whole episode with Rafe made me examine myself and my habits. I don't think I can afford to drink casually. Anyway, I don't want to risk it. I need a clear head."

"You aren't the least like Rafael St. John! But I won't push you. It's entirely your decision."

"Thank you, Harry," Catherine said ironically.

There was no one else in the lounge, so he took advantage of the fact and kissed her lingeringly. She wove her arms around his neck and kissed him back. Sometimes she thought she might die without Harry. How Daphne Binoche could waltz in and out of relationships, Catherine couldn't understand.

* * *

The following morning, Catherine woke, showered, and walked to the diner where she had oatmeal with brown sugar and blueberries. Harry joined her halfway through her breakfast.

"Max rang. He's coming along after our seminars to take us to the beach this afternoon. I think the break will do us good."

"Oh!" Catherine said, "How splendid! Jolly good thing I brought my bathing costume."

Harry raised his eyebrows. "Now that I cannot wait to see! That reminds me. Max said there is nothing as civilized as bathing huts. You'll have to wear your costume under your clothes to and from the beach. Still game?"

"I am!"

* * *

This morning's seminar had eight new girls, with the subject matter still the same as Tuesday's. When she went over her new students' roll, one name particularly caught her eye: Alvira Fields. Her interest was piqued. That was the name of Michael Fields's daughter, wasn't it?

When the students arrived and sat at their desks, she sought to improve on Tuesday's situation by asking them to introduce themselves and tell the group what they were studying. Alvira turned out to be a stunning blonde with shoulder-length hair and eyes the color of blueberries.

"I want to become an actress," she said, impressing Catherine with her self-possession. "Probably a stage actress. My mother acts on Broadway."

"How interesting," said Catherine. "I have always loved stage productions. I wish you the best of luck."

The other girls wanted to be writers or "go to New York and work in publishing."

Catherine was impressed. These California girls had more ambition than she was used to seeing. Other than Dot, most of the women she had known in college had taken their degrees home with them and concentrated on making a good marriage.

"Well, it seems that it would help all of you to have a solid foundation in Modern English Literature. I expect we will have some lively discussions." She gave her pre-War/post-War presentation and said that from that day forth, the class format would be discussion. She gave the same reading and writing assignment to these girls she had given to the Tuesday group.

When class was over, she asked Michael Fields' daughter to stay behind for a moment.

"I am very sorry for your recent loss, Miss Fields. I am looking into your father's death for MGM. It seems Louis Mayer is old-fashioned and doesn't have much faith in the police."

"Is this some kind of gig Oxford professors do on the side?" the girl asked.

Catherine laughed. "Dr. Bascombe and I sort of fell into it. We were wrongly accused of murder last year. The police weren't getting anywhere, so we decided to take a hand in the investigation. Much to their chagrin. Since then, we've had a hand in solving a couple of other cases."

The girl studied Catherine as though weighing her mentally. She said, "Bizarre. But I don't think you're needed in this instance. My father's mistress is guilty. What more is there to find out?" the girl said. "She's been arrested."

Catherine had known this was going to be difficult. It was an extremely awkward position. "I understand how this whole thing must make you feel, but Miss Binoche denies that she was your father's mistress. There have also been several attempts on *her* life."

Alvira Fields rooted through her schoolbag and produced a pack of cigarettes and a lighter, managing to look worldly-wise. "Please. My father worshipped her." Rolling her eyes, she lit her cigarette and took a deep drag. "And it would be just like her to make up tales of someone trying to kill her. I've met her. She's a complete neurotic."

"Why would she kill your father?"

"Because he was old-fashioned. He wouldn't divorce my mother. She probably worked herself up into some sort of frenzy and then lost her head and shot him. I can see it happening that way quite easily."

Unfortunately, Catherine could picture that as well. She tried once more. "You know of no one else with a motive?"

"Well, he did have a detective looking into something for him. Lionel and I saw them together. Li recognized him. Phil something. I don't remember."

"Lionel?" Catherine asked.

"My boyfriend. He's an actor. He's fabulous. I was trying to get Dad to get Li a role in a new Western he knew about. Now, of course, that won't happen. Poor Lionel. But he'll get his big break soon. He has to."

Catherine wondered what Michael Fields had really thought of Lionel's acting skills and if the boyfriend could be another suspect. "I'd like to meet Lionel," she said. "Maybe he could join you after class someday. Do the two of you ever go to the Starlight Club?"

"Dad got us in there occasionally. We haven't been since he's been . . . gone."

For the first time, the girl's sophisticated mask slipped, and she had the forlorn look of a child who has lost its parent.

"I'm so sorry, Miss Fields. I won't keep you any longer. Could you just ring me at the Westwood Inn if you remember anything else that might be helpful?"

"I suppose so. It's going to be really strange having you for a teacher," the student said.

Catherine agreed. "If it becomes too strange, you can always withdraw from the class, but I hope it doesn't come to that. I'd like to get to know you better."

"Why?"

Catherine smiled. "I like having curious, intelligent women to teach."

"I'll give it a week," the girl said. "The reading sounds good, at least. I'm off to the bookstore to buy the novels." Alvira Fields stopped when she reached the door of the classroom and turned. "Please don't bother my mother with questions. She is struggling terribly over the loss of my father."

Catherine just nodded, but she was surprised. Ruth Delano Fields had apparently put on an act for her daughter. Catherine didn't think women who were devastated by their husbands' deaths would be entering into new intimacies with the carefree abandon Miss Fields's mother had shown. But then what did Catherine know about Hollywood?

* * *

It was good to see "Cowboy" Max again. After meeting so many strong personalities in such a short space of time, she had become immersed in Hollywood. It was refreshing to be with someone who wasn't putting on an act.

They took the Chevrolet, and Max made his way to the Pacific Coast Highway, which took them along the ocean. Catherine thought it was the same way she and Harry had driven the day before when they followed the Pierce-Arrow, but then she had been keeping her eye on the sports car. Once they got past the vast San Pedro and Long Beach Harbors and the ugly oil wells thinned out, the sparsely frequented beaches were made of fine, nearly white sand that extended on for miles. The Pacific was different from the choppy Atlantic she saw out from Cornwall. It was blue, and the horizon was free of mist thanks to the heat, so one could see further. And there were the magnificent waves which Max called breakers.

He kept driving south—away from the populated shore until they came to an empty stretch that seemed to go on forever named Huntington Beach. They parked the Chevrolet and took their towels, and walked out over the hot white sand. It was even more beautiful to her than the famous Cote d'Azur where she had holidayed in the past.

They chose a place to stretch out their towels, and Catherine self-consciously stripped off her blouse and skirt, revealing her bathing costume.

"My, my," said Harry. "What have we here?"

"Don't," said Catherine, hastily sitting on her towel and rolling over so her back was to him. "You make me entirely too self-conscious."

"Well, then. Anyone for a bathe?" asked Harry, stepping out of his outer clothes.

"Not until I'm all warmed up," said Catherine.

"I'll go," said Max. "You really need to swim in pairs. There's sometimes a riptide that pulls you out to sea before you know it. I'll show you how to swim in the waves."

The two of them went off for their bathe, and Catherine promptly fell asleep in the sun. She had a glorious nap until Harry turned up and began dripping saltwater over her.

"Up, up, sleepyhead. Come cast your cares upon the great waters! It is jolly great fun!"

Irritably, she sat up, forgetting how exposed she was. Catherine felt hot and sticky and ready for a swim. Taking to her heels, she ran straight into the sea. It seemed cold, but the temperature was welcome. She walked further out and was surprised how steeply the bottom fell away. Soon she was swimming towards the breakers. When one crashed down upon her, she was tossed about in the surge and then thrown up upon the sand.

Catherine coughed up seawater. Max and Harry laughed.

"Come along," said Harry. "We'll show you how it's done."

After about twenty minutes of instruction, she was "catching" the waves with her body and "riding" them to shore. It was great fun, and she completely forgot that Michael Fields had been murdered.

Once she sat down on her towel and began to rub her hair dry, Max, who was digging a purposeless hole in the sand, asked, his voice diffident, "Is Dot dating anyone these days?"

Catherine's antennae quivered. Was Max still interested in Dot? Her friend had gone through a rough bit when she had heard he was engaged. The initial reason for this trip had been so they could see each other.

"No one exclusively," Catherine said. Actually, Dot had found British men couldn't measure up to her "cowboy." Max was his own breed.

His face flushed. "My fiancée and I are going through a rough patch," he said. "She's pretty sure she doesn't want to leave Julesburg even to go to Chicago."

"I'm sorry to hear that," Catherine said. "Dot will be, too. She cares about your happiness."

"I care about hers, as well. That's why I finally went and got engaged to an American girl. I can't see Dot living here after

London. But now I've found myself with the opposite problem. The two women are as different as they can be."

"Dot loves adventure first and foremost. Did you ever talk to her about it?"

He shrugged and started filling in his hole.

For a moment, things were awkward, and then she remembered she had a question to ask Max.

"This was a jolly good idea, Max! I say, I was just wondering, do you know Del Fields? He's the murdered man's son. He goes to UCLA."

"Relax, darling," said Harry. "Forget about the murder for a while. This is the holiday part of our trip."

"As a matter of fact, I do know the young Fields," said Max. "We both belong to EPIC."

"What is that? It sounds like a film company," said Catherine. "I didn't know you were interested in the pictures, Max."

Max laughed. "No. Not even close. It's a political organization: End Poverty in California."

"That sounds terrifically high-minded and noble," said Harry.

"It is. We haven't had a terrific amount of success so far, though. Have you ever heard of the American writer, Upton Sinclair?" Catherine knew she had had too much sun. She began pulling her clothes on over her bathing costume. "Isn't he a novelist? I can't remember what he wrote at the moment, but I do remember it causing a bit of a sensation."

"*The Jungle*. At least that's the book Sinclair's famous for. It's an exposé of the horrible conditions in the meatpacking industry. He's what the Americans call a muckraker. A socialist dedicated to reform," said Max. "I kind of got on his bandwagon because of the meatpacking plant where our ranch sends our beef. We send it by train down here to Southern California. It's an awful place. Almost put me off meat."

"I see," said Catherine. "But you said there hasn't been a terrific amount of success?"

"Well, Mr. Sinclair ran for governor last year on a Socialist ticket.

EPIC was the organization behind his campaign. Unfortunately, he lost. Now we're working on getting Robert Henlein, another author, elected to the California State Assembly. There are a lot of movie star types who belong and do fundraising for us. We also write articles and organize protests. Anything to help people see the poverty here in Southern California. We have 700,000 people out of work here in the state with the Depression."

"How awful. But how marvelous that you're working to help, Max," said Catherine.

"Don't tell me you're going to forsake your education and go into politics," said Harry.

"No. Though Dickens was a bit of a muckraker, you know."

"He was a silly romantic. Loved to write the sob stuff," said Harry. "I can't abide him."

"Oh, Harry, put a sock in it," she scolded, batting him with her hand. "Don't get him going on about Dickens," she warned Max.

"I heard that Del was a Communist. EPIC is probably a little tame for him," Max said.

"Now that's interesting!" said Harry. "I shouldn't wonder if he had differences with his father over that. The professor told us that Del's grandfather was a wealthy industrialist. That's where the family money comes from."

Taking a comb out of her purse, Catherine began trying to comb surf and sand out of her hair, wishing again for a bathing hut.

"There's another group called the Anti-Nazi League that Del's a member of. I suspect it's definitely a front organization for the Communist Party, though it claims to be just an Anti-Nazi group. There are a bunch of movie stars affiliated with it, too."

Pulling a jumper over his head, Max continued, "Everyone is het up over what the Fascists are doing in Spain and Germany. There are a lot of Jews in Hollywood, and they aren't happy with the persecution that's going on in Europe. You'd be surprised how many of them have become Communists."

Catherine scowled as she tried to untangle her hair. "Let me help you." Harry took the comb from her and gently worked it through her hair, starting at the ends. It was a surprisingly intimate gesture. She gave herself up to the pleasure.

"That sounds interesting," said Catherine. "But when all is said and done, Communism is pretty extreme in the leftist direction. It may have inured Del to things like murder." Catherine had a good friend, Red, who headed a jazz band in Oxford. He was a dedicated Communist, and they had gone the rounds about this topic more than once.

"We have an EPIC meeting tonight at the Los Angeles library if you want to meet Del," said Max. "I think you'll be impressed. He's got his father's presence about him."

"Well, if we're going to do that, I have to get back to the inn and do my hair," she said, looking at Harry as she put on her cartwheel sun hat. "Thank you, darling, for trying to undo the damage."

"What time does it start?" Harry asked.

"Not 'til nine. We have time. We can pick up some fresh crab and take it back with us. I can boil it up in my apartment. Nothing like fresh crab."

"That sounds lovely," said Catherine. "But I do have to spend some time on my hair."

They stopped for the crab at a shack along the coast highway and made it back to Westwood by five o'clock. Catherine wondered if she would ever get used to the open spaces of the American West.

* * *

The L.A. Public Library was the first public building in Los Angeles Catherine had seen that made an attempt at grandeur. It gave the nod to Egypt with the bas reliefs over the main entrance. When they got to the meeting room, which was quite large, they mingled with distinguished looking men in light-colored suits and women in expensive-looking linen frocks. It was still a bit warm, and the windows were open and overhead fans going. Catherine looked around, hoping she could spot a movie star or two, but she had no luck.

There were no chairs. People just stood about in groups and conversed. All that was missing were the cocktails. Catherine was extremely glad Max was with them. He pointed out would-be Assemblyman Henlein and liberal organizer Melvyn Douglas. Donation envelopes were handed around.

Finally, a young man with a dimple in his chin and flaxen hair which fell over his forehead banged a gavel and the business portion of the evening began.

"That's Del," Max whispered to her, speaking of the man with the gavel who was now giving the most recent unemployment figures. They were bad, but he said he had some good news.

"Harry Hopkins—yes, the same Harry Hopkins who is a close associate of FDR—has visited us this week. He had heard of our program for End Poverty in California and has said that FDR is most interested in including it in his own Federal Relief Program. So we are making a difference, ladies and gentlemen! I would encourage you all to contribute generously to our cause and to recruit other members.

"Now we will have a few words from Robert Henlein, who has decided to run for the California State Assembly. He will speak to you about his agenda. Many of you work in high places. We encourage you and everyone to spread the word about our candidate. This time we will succeed and end up with a loud voice in Sacramento."

After the Henlein speech, which wasn't nearly as passionate as Del's, the business portion of the evening was over. Several comely young ladies came around to collect the envelopes, and men began producing their hip flasks to have a tipple.

Max told them to stay where they were, and he moved off in the crowd. To Harry and Catherine's satisfaction, he eventually returned with Del Fields.

Max said, "Del, these are my professor friends from Oxford, Dr. Bascombe and Miss Tregowyn. They're teaching at UCLA this summer. They're interested in talking to you further about the movement. Harry, Catherine, this is Mr. Delano Fields."

The crowd was loud, and Fields was regrettably distracted. He was not as young as Catherine expected, and Catherine decided he must be taking longer than the standard four years to get through university.

Harry said, "We have some time free tomorrow. I'm hearing good things about the Brown Derby. Could we meet there at 1:00? We'd like to stand you lunch and hear more."

Fields was only too happy to acquiesce. He shook hands on it and then moved away, brushing his hair back from his brow with a gesture that spoke to Catherine of his drama-prone Mama.

Chapter Eleven

Catherine woke the following day with the sensation that she had forgotten something important. She went over all the events of the day before. Class, the beach, the EPIC meeting. She was forgetting something! She went over everything again, accounting for all the blocs of the day's activities. Then she had it.

She had forgotten Alvira! Catherine got out of bed and sorted her clothes for the laundry. Concentrating on yesterday's conversation, she tried to recall everything that was said. She remembered "Li" or Lionel. What was it Lionel had told Alvira? Phil. Who was Phil?

She raced to the telephone and called Harry's room.

"Darling, I forgot something that could be important."

"Good morning to you, too," Harry said. She could hear the grin in his voice.

"Harry! This is important. I think I have a lead. Alvira, Michael Fields' daughter, is in my class. She spoke to me afterward, and she told me that a detective was quote hanging around before her father died. Don't you think that's strange?"

"Very. It could be important. I don't suppose she gave you a name?"

"Phil. Short for Phillip, I imagine." Catherine absently noted a ladder in one of her stockings.

Harry said, "I've got a telephone book here in the room. I'll look up detectives. You don't suppose she meant a police detective, do you?"

"No. I don't think so. I think she would have just called him the 'police.'"

"All right, I've got 'detectives,' and it says 'see private investigators.' Give me half a mo.'" Catherine heard the pages rustle.

"Got it!" he said. "All right. Phillip. Yes, I've found him! There's a Phillip Black. Figueroa Street, Los Angeles."

"It's too early, still to call him," Catherine said, noting it was only 7:30.

"I think this would be handled better in person than on the telephone," said Harry. "I'll call at 8:00 and try to make an appointment for this morning."

"All right. I'll be right here. I'm just doing chores."

All the time Catherine sorted laundry, trimmed and varnished her fingernails, and washed the sand from her bathing costume; she wondered if they were only minutes away from solving the crime.

Harry told her they had a 10:00 appointment. Dressing with care, she tried to look professional in her white linen suit with her red and white blouse. She donned her white cloche hat just before Harry knocked on her door.

"Darling, you look every inch the private secretary," said Harry.

"I hope I will do. You look very smart."

"Thank you. Shall we?" he offered his arm, which she took.

Figueroa Street proved to be right in downtown Los Angeles. They found the street without trouble. The detective's office was on the third floor of a three-story office building with no lift. By the time they reached the upper floor, Catherine was feeling the heat indeed. She stopped to powder her face.

A Miss Minton—red-haired and red-faced—asked them to wait in the chairs provided.

"Mr. Black will only be a moment. My, I like your hat, Mrs. Bascombe. Where did you buy it, may I ask?"

"London, I'm afraid," said Catherine with a smile. "We're visiting from England."

"Oh! Are you on vacation?"

"Work, I'm afraid," said Catherine.

Catherine could tell the woman very much wanted to ask what sort of work she did, and Catherine didn't seem to think there was any harm in it, so she said, "We teach at UCLA."

At that moment, Mr. Phillip Black became available and showed them into his office. The man was short and thick with a Clark Gable mustache and a cigar stub in his mouth. His face was tanned and seamed as though he had seen a difficult life.

"Now," he said, his voice brisk. "What can I do for you folks?"

Harry introduced the two of them and then said, "You are in a position to help us quite a lot with our investigation. As you know, one of your clients was shot and killed—Mr. Michael Fields."

The detective took the cigarette out of his mouth and set it in the ashtray, still burning. "You're detectives? You sure don't look like it."

"We're interested parties. A friend of ours is under arrest for the crime. We think that the work you did for Mr. Fields may lead us to the real murderer."

"Well, then, I'm sorry. Real sorry. But that work was confidential. I can't tell you. It wouldn't do if my other clients found out ol' Phil Black was givin' away confidential information."

Harry and Catherine sighed in unison. Harry said, "And if the police applied to you with a warrant?"

"Now, that might be a different story. Depends upon the wording of that warrant. I don't hold with fishing expeditions. Now, I'm real sorry, folks, but I'm going to have to ask you to leave now. I'm sorry you had this trip downtown for nothin.'"

"Not as sorry as we are," said Catherine.

* * *

When they returned to the inn to await their luncheon with Del, Catherine called the maid service to pick up her laundry. As she waited in the sitting room, she had plenty of time to think about what she knew. Michael Fields was emerging as a busy man and an absent husband and father. Fancy having an apartment when you had that huge house just miles away! She suspected he had a very separate life from the rest of his family. There were germs of dissension between all its members.

She knew she had to get into that apartment. Perhaps Daphne had a key.

After the maid left with her clothes, Catherine opened the small notebook she kept in her purse and wrote herself a reminder about the key. She noted other questions she had written there.

What if Fields had tried to separate his daughter from her beloved Lionel because he was a terrible actor and had no future?

What if the detective Lionel had recognized was actually investigating Ruth Delano Fields to find evidence of adultery so he could divorce her? If not, what did he hire him to do?

How long had Ruth's affair been going on with Calloway? Did Calloway murder Fields so he wouldn't divorce Ruth and separate her from a healthy inheritance?

What if Fields had threatened his son, Del? Said that he would cut him out of his will if he didn't cease dallying with Communists?

Catherine had little to go on, but she still couldn't make up her mind about Daphne, either. Her performance the other day had had the effect of making Catherine wary of her and loathe to believe anything she said. And she was wary of Buck, as well.

One thing was for certain. Currents ran deep here. Catherine knew there were things she hadn't begun to grasp. It was highly frustrating, and she had no clue what to do about it.

Where was Buck when the murder took place? How many people knew about Fields' apartment and its location?

Ruth Delano Fields most certainly did. If her daughter was to be believed, she still had feelings for her husband, though she didn't want him or anyone to know. Did she love him or hate him?

Perhaps both? Was the affair with Calloway payback for what she imagined to be his affair with Daphne? Maybe their relationship was too complex for Catherine to begin to understand.

Maybe Dr. Adler would have some psychological insights based on what he'd witnessed. Was he still at Buck's?

From what little she had seen of Alvira, she couldn't imagine her shooting her father, but Catherine hadn't met Lionel yet. Surely his girlfriend's inheritance would come in handy until he "got his break."

And Del was another story. He was a driven personality who struck her as someone who would never let anyone or anything stand in his way. She would have to see what he had to say when they met for lunch.

Richard Darcy probably knew everything there was to know about all the people involved in this situation. But as things stood, the known facts didn't eliminate anyone she had met. Going to the gossipmonger seemed underhanded, but she was ready to try anything that would give her a more clear vision of what she needed to see. Catherine knew she knew she needed facts, however. Not innuendo.

* * *

"Where did you hear about the Brown Derby?" Catherine asked Harry as they pulled up to a parking place next to the restaurant. To her disbelief, it was shaped like a Brown Derby hat.

"I asked Max where there was a restaurant to get a good steak. I figured a cattle rancher would know," said Harry.

"It's certainly original looking."

"Very California, that's for certain."

The inside of the restaurant was far more traditional, with wooden paneling and white linen tablecloths. There were also caricatures of movie stars adorning the walls, leading Catherine to believe they had stumbled on a Hollywood institution.

Harry had made a reservation, so they were shown right to

their table for three. Harry ordered a whiskey, Catherine tonic water. Del was late, apparently.

"So," Harry said. "Who do you think killed Michael Fields?"

"I've no idea," said Catherine. "Not a sausage."

"I rather fancy going to the Starlight Club again tonight if we can get Buck to take us."

"Harry! You have a lecture!"

"That will be over by nine. I imagine that's just when things get cookin' as they say in America."

"Do you know how to get in touch with Buck?"

"He gave me his number. I'll ring him before the lecture. He's probably on the set this afternoon."

Finally, Del breezed in, his blond hair falling over his brow again. He was dressed in working-class clothes—a gray cotton shirt and trousers, but he had added a navy blue tie, so he met the restaurant's standards.

"Hello," he greeted them. "I'm sorry, I know it's awfully rude, but I've forgotten your names. I just recognized you by sight."

"I'm Catherine Tregowyn." She offered her hand to the student.

"Harry Bascombe." Harry shook hands with the man, saying, "And you're Delano Fields,"

"Del. And I'm hungry. Great of you to offer me a meal. Must confess I haven't eaten since yesterday's lunch. Too much to do."

The waiter appeared, and Del ordered a beer. They all ordered steak and French fries.

"I expected you to be a vegetarian with your connection to Upton Sinclair and *The Jungle*," said Catherine.

He looked at her blankly for a moment, then smiled. "Don't have a comeback for that, sorry. I love steak. And actually, they hand butcher it here."

Catherine wrinkled her nose. "I didn't need to know that."

"So." He looked from one of them to the other. "You know Max."

"Yes," said Harry. "He studied with me last year at Oxford.

He's the one behind our being here. He wanted us to teach a summer course at UCLA, and he must have some sort of connections, because here we are."

"We're very interested in your work to end poverty," said Catherine disingenuously. "As you can imagine, this is a serious problem in Britain, as well. Tell us what you do besides supporting political candidates."

His whole visage brightened. "Well, as you heard last night, we've caught the attention of the White House. They're going to implement some of our ideas in the Federal program. This is a huge opportunity for us. We've proposed a public works initiative." He continued talking about the EPIC ideas, which were in consideration by Harry Hopkins and FDR.

"That's fascinating," said Harry, who was, in fact, a political conservative. "Certainly much better than simply handing people the money. If they work for it, they'll handle it better."

"That's the hope."

"Max told us you were also a member of the Communist Party," said Harry.

"That's true."

"Your mother says you play baseball," said Catherine. "I admit, it's a little bit of a stretch to think of you doing both."

"Wait, you know my mother?" he said.

Catherine realized her error and backtracked. "We met her with a group of theater people," she said.

"But she never talks about her children!"

"I asked her if she had any at UCLA. That's how I heard about the baseball."

"Me? Baseball? You've got to be joking! I can't imagine where she got that idea. All the spare time I have from studying is taken up with EPIC."

Del didn't realize it, but he'd just jettisoned his alibi. And his mother's. But then he didn't even know they knew about his father and his murder.

Catherine said, "I was appalled to hear about your father's murder."

"Please accept our condolences," said Harry. "That must be very difficult."

Del's face hardened. "Of course, I'm sorry that he's dead, but he and I were like oil and water. He cut me off completely last month."

She was longing to ask about his father's estate but didn't have the nerve.

Del was clenching and unclenching his right hand. His face had gone red. Catherine wondered if he scorned inherited wealth. Didn't the Communists abhor that? She knew her friend, Red, had forsaken his noble status and the family estate when he became a Communist.

They ate the delicious steak and potatoes in silence for a few minutes. Catherine finally said, "I understand there are quite a few Communists in the film community. Because of their Anti-Nazi stance. We had a terrible scandal at Oxford about a secret Fascist community among the faculty and students who were terrorizing Jews."

"Hmm," said Del. "Have no time for Fascists. Hitler's going to start a war. That'll just about finish Europe, I guess. But when the old ways are torn down, there will be more room for the new."

Harry grinned. "Sounds like you're a bit of an anarchist."

Del remained serious. "Whatever it takes. Speaking of Fascists, I just met a friend of my father's yesterday." Frowning, he cut a piece of meat. "He has only been here a couple of months and didn't know about my political affiliation."

Del chewed thoughtfully before continuing. "The man is a genuine Nazi. He even admitted it. Trying to get Daryl Zanuck—our only non-Jewish movie mogul—to do an epic feature on the American West. He says the Cowboy is the quintessential Aryan role model."

"Golly, we'll have to tell Max," said Catherine with a grin. "We have a friend who is a cowboy."

"It's not a laughing matter," said Del. He leaned forward on his elbows, his voice down, his eyes glowing with intensity. "We don't need his sort in Hollywood. Hitler's rise to power is being documented by a powerful director. Have you ever heard of Leni Riefenstahl? She's a dangerous person. I think she could sell snow to an Eskimo. She has demonstrated what a political tool film can be."

"What do you plan to do about it?" asked Harry.

"The Anti-Nazi League is keeping an eye on him. We've also petitioned Daryl Zanuck to no avail. I think he's going ahead with the film."

Catherine could see that Del was completely serious. She asked, "Did he ever pitch your father about this film? What's his name, by the way?"

"Helmut Grossman. And yes, he did pitch my father. Dad was actually considering it. I was pretty incensed, I can tell you, but my father and I didn't get along, so it was no use talking to him. He just thought it was my Communist prejudice. He couldn't see the project for what it was. I couldn't even get into see Louis Mayer, so that was a bust."

Catherine looked at Harry over the rim of her glass as she took a sip.

Harry drew him out with questions of how he had made the political decisions he had, which took up the remainder of their lunchtime. Finally, just as Del was making noises about how he ought to go, Harry asked, "Have you any more meetings coming up?"

"The ANL meets on Saturday night. Anti-Nazi League. It's a bit further to the left than EPIC. We're watchdogs. Many of the members are Communists."

"Sounds interesting," said Harry. "Where and when?"

"The Public Library. Same room. 9:00 p.m. It's a good meeting for you to come to because it's Recruit Night."

"Maybe we'll see you then," said Harry.

Del rose. "Thanks for lunch. He took a tablet out of his shirt pocket and wrote something down. As he handed it to Harry, he said, "Here's my number if you ever need to get in touch with me."

The young man walked out of the restaurant, his stride purposeful.

"Communists may not eat apple pie," said Harry. "But I do. We're in America, after all."

Catherine said, "The boy doesn't realize he's got a tremendous motive. Money. The best motive there is.

* * *

Harry's lecture on the author's psychological profiles revealed in the Brontë sisters' literature went over exceptionally well. Catherine had never seen Harry lecture before and was delighted at his wit and urbanity. He had the audience eating out of his hand.

Mr. Darcy was as good as his word, and the audience was packed with community members who seemed to look upon Harry as another entertainer. He didn't let them down, and Catherine suspected he could have held his own against any Hollywood type.

Dr. Adler was present, as were Daphne, Buck, Lady Naomi, and surprisingly Hyacinth. Catherine joined them in the queue, waiting to congratulate Harry. They were all dressed for an evening out. Catherine had worn her linen suit, conscious of her scholarly role.

"What is your verdict, Professor?" asked Catherine.

"For an amateur psychologist, it was excellent. I, of course, as a student of Freud, would like to have known more about the mother."

Catherine smiled. "Of course you would. Harry feels that that is his one great gap, but little is known about her. All that he knows is simply inferred from the absence of a good mother image in the sisters' works. Mrs. Reed in Jane Eyre is certainly a fearsome creature."

"Well, I thought it was smashing," said Lady Naomi. "Harry is a success at whatever he undertakes."

"It sounds like you know him well," said Hyacinth.

"Eons. Years ago, when we were at school. Harry and I had a thing. He was frightfully upset when I ended things."

Buck asked, "Catherine, will you and Harry join us tonight at the Starlight Club? We are making an all-out effort to cheer Daphne."

"Certainly," said Catherine. "But I shall have to go back to the Inn first to put on my glad rags."

When they finally made it to the front of the queue, Harry was startled to see all of them there. "Wouldn't they let you in at the Starlight tonight?" he asked.

"We're going there after," said Hyacinth. "You're to come, too." She fluttered her eyelashes. "You're the very best dancing partner I've ever had. I'm counting on you!"

Harry looked over at Catherine. "Yes!" she said.

* * *

"Darling, you were fabulous," said Catherine on the way back to the inn. "I feel you may have missed your calling. Perhaps you belong in Hollywood after all."

"I turned it up a notch tonight, I must confess," said Harry with a laugh. "But thank you. I'm rather afraid that Darcy fellow is going to go over the top on his broadcast. He was embarrassingly complimentary."

"Perhaps you had better see if the university has a bigger hall for your next lecture."

"It's your turn to perform next!"

"Crikey!" she said. "I'll never match your star power!"

"Stuff! You're so lovely to look at; you will have excelled before you utter your first sentence."

"Harry! You know I have to succeed on my academic merits!"

"Well, that's true, but beauty never hurts. Just ask Buck," said Harry as they pulled into the Inn.

"What?"

"He's got a pash for you, I'm afraid," said Harry ruefully.

"Darling, you know he's completely gone on Daphne. Besides, how could he ever compare to anyone who can run on as exquisitely as you do?"

She was making fun, of course, but the truth was that no one she had met—including her longtime former love, Rafe—had ever been able to compare to Harry. As time passed, she became more aware of that, and it even frightened her a little. Underneath the banter, there was a passionate connection between her and Dr. Harry.

Of course, it hadn't started out that way. She always smiled when she remembered how angry he had been at her for publishing the biography of his own "mystery poet," whom he had been on the track of for years. They had undoubtedly gotten off on the wrong foot! But then they had discovered a body together, and the rest was history.

Thinking fondly of these things, she dressed in an ice blue cocktail frock with a white feather boa. It was a good thing her hair was behaving, for she didn't have the time or the inclination to fuss with it now. After outlining her eyes with kohl, she carefully applied a new pink lipstick.

CHAPTER TWELVE

The Starlight Club was alive with jazz and laughter when Harry and Catherine arrived and gave Buck's name to the bouncer. The actor came over to claim them.

"Glad you could make it! We've got a terrific band tonight. Gerry Knight is on the sax. He's becoming a legend here in Hollywood."

As soon as they reached Buck's table, they saw that all the habitues were there, including Daphne, who sat drinking what looked like whiskey. Catherine wouldn't have taken her for a whiskey drinker, but then she wouldn't have picked her for a Communist, either.

Lady Naomi rose to collect Harry. "Oh, darling, I remember what a splendid dancer you are," she said, leading a clearly reluctant Harry out on the dance floor. "I've been so longing for you to arrive."

Catherine knew Harry had just been teasing about Buck, who was clearly devoted to Daphne, but she was rather annoyed when the actor swept her out on the dance floor without so much as a by your leave. He moved her smoothly away from the table into a foxtrot.

She soon surrendered herself to the lively tune. Why was she so wary of the classically handsome man with his smooth charm? It was more than just being confused about his origins. Something about him just seemed off.

"How is Daphne carrying on?" she asked her partner.

"Badly. The press has been hounding her."

"Surely they're not allowed in here!"

"That idiot, Richard Darcy, has a membership."

She scanned the room. "Yes," said Catherine. "He's sitting next to Daphne, isn't he? Perhaps Harry will divert him. I understand we have Mr. Darcy to thank for the interest in Harry's lecture tonight."

"Yes. Darcy's basking in its success, as a matter of fact," Buck said. "Saying he's made a new discovery."

"He seems an odd fellow."

"Publicity mad. He doesn't have the looks to be an actor, so he hides behind the radio." Buck's comment was quite obviously smug. "Harry was entertaining tonight. You've got hold of a good thing, there."

"I think so," she said. "He's a very gifted lecturer."

"Hmm," said Buck. "I don't suppose I could interest you in dinner out with me one evening?"

His invitation threw her, his forwardness making her uncomfortable. Catherine had no doubt that there was an angle. What did he have to say that he couldn't right now? Her immediate reaction was to say no. But then she realized that Buck could be very helpful in their investigation if he chose. He knew the players. And they hadn't ruled him out as a murderer.

"I would enjoy that," she found herself saying. "I don't think Harry would mind." That was an out and out lie. Harry would be very worried about her safety.

"Tomorrow night, then?"

"An early dinner would be lovely. Harry and I have an engagement at nine," she said.

"I will call for you at six-thirty, then. You're at the Westwood Inn?"

"Yes." Catherine decided to make use of this opportunity for a tête-à-tête. "Could you tell me what you know about Joseph Callaway?"

"So he's caught your eye, is that it?"

"Let's just say that I learned something about him that made me regard him in a new light."

"Well, he's got more money than Midas. Inherited it, I think. And though one wouldn't think it with his saturnine looks, women like him."

"Maybe it's the money," Catherine said with a bit of a laugh.

"Could be. He keeps two residences—one a ways away down the coast where he gives parties and such. Most of the time, he lives in a nice little apartment. Same building as Fields, as a matter of fact."

"Hmm," said Catherine.

"You know, I find it very uncanny that someone as lovely as you is an actual sleuth."

"Flattery will get you everywhere," she said. "Thank you, sir."

The dance ended, and Buck returned her to her table. She was enjoying dancing as an instrument of interrogation. It was working well for her.

As soon as Buck had left to get her a tonic water, Richard Darcy pounced. "My dear Miss Tregowyn! If you listen to my radio show tomorrow morning at 8:00 a.m., you will hear my review of Dr. Bascombe's lecture. I shall give your lecture a promo. The information you gave me said that you were going to speak on the War Poets and that Dr. Bascombe was going to do readings?"

"Yes," said Catherine. "That's the plan. As you can imagine, he's very good at it."

Mr. Darcy laughed and said, "He had better take care, or one of the studios will try to pressure him into a contract. He has a Douglas Fairbanks, Jr. look to him. I daresay he could make a lot more money in films."

Even though Catherine was very aware of that, she said, "Harry is very happy at Oxford. I don't think Hollywood would suit him."

Mr. Darcy looked at her in astonishment, his sparse eyebrows near his blond hairline. "He would rather teach college students in damp old Britain, bless Her, than lead the glamorous and comfortable life of a Hollywood film star?"

"Well, you can certainly ask him," she said, comfortable in the knowledge that she was right. Buck appeared at her side, beverage in hand.

Richard Darcy continued. "He looks to be enthralled with Lady Naomi. Now *there* is an interesting woman."

Catherine smiled, refusing to take the bait. "Yes. She has made quite a splash in dull, damp old Britain."

"I can only imagine."

She added, "She and Harry were chums when they were undergraduates. Did you know that she took a first in Modern Languages? She speaks five, I think."

"Does she now? How very intriguing." He brought his hand up to his chin and ran the index finger across his mouth, mentally cooking up something, no doubt.

"Bascombe regretted that he did not have time to be interviewed on my broadcast, but perhaps Lady Naomi would be an even bigger draw," he said. "I understand she shoots lions and flies airplanes."

"I imagine she would adore being interviewed," said Catherine, grateful that Harry had declined. She took a sip of her drink and then shifted topics. Pleased that the man oozed egotism, she decided to dig a bit. "Mr. Darcy, You must be in a very good position to know these people better than anyone. I would love to hear your impressions of Michael Fields."

The man's eyes lit even in the semi-darkness. "Oh yes. I knew Mr. Fields quite well. Brilliant man with just that unique kink that made him stand out from other directors. He had a singular vision. It is a terrible loss."

Catherine wet her lips with the tonic water. "I, personally, can't believe Miss Binoche guilty. What do you think?"

"Oh, I don't think Daphne has the grit to kill anyone. She is a very inward-looking person, you know. That's what makes her such a fine actress."

"What can you tell me about Del Fields? He seems an interesting young man," she said.

"Ah . . . I'm not going to talk about Del. It would be indiscreet of me," he surprised Catherine by saying.

He appeared to be about to say something further, but at that moment, Joe Calloway interrupted them.

"How is your ankle, Miss Tregowyn?" He extended a hand.

"All well, thank you." She regretted the intrusion, but lest she leave Mr. Darcy with the impression that she was unbecomingly interested in the murder, she turned her attention to the actor. She had a difficult time seeing him as a playboy.

"Would you care to try dancing with me again?" he asked. "I found I enjoyed it the other night."

She didn't care to, but she knew she ought to. Excusing herself to Mr. Darcy, she took the floor with Joe Calloway.

"Harry was just telling us all about how you sang with a jazz band," he said. "And here I thought you were this repressed literature professor."

Stunned, she said, "What on earth gave you that idea? About the repressed part, I mean."

"Actually, it was something Lady Naomi said, though I can't remember what. Very vague. You know the sort of thing. Seeming to feel so sorry for you, but really stabbing you in the back."

Catherine bristled. With an effort, she placed what she hoped was a pleasant smile on her face. "I could have gone all night without hearing that, Mr. Calloway," she said, her voice sweet as honey.

"Well, I thought you ought to beware. She means to steal Harry out from under your nose."

Catherine laughed. "She thrives on competition."

"You seem very confident," the actor said.

"I'm very British," she said. "But I'm not enjoying this conversation, Mr. Calloway. I suggest you find another topic. Maybe I can help. Let's talk about something more interesting. Murder, for instance."

He smiled his villain's smile, showing too many teeth. "I'd be happy to. Michael was not really a pleasant person, you know."

This was a surprise. "Really?"

"Oh, he had something that drove the women wild, but he was a cold-hearted fellow. Being such a great director, he had an instinct about what made people tick, and he didn't hesitate to use it against them."

Is there another motive here?

"He does sound dashed unpleasant. Can you give me an example?"

"He was the expert at promising things he had no intention of delivering. I was to just hold out for one more picture, and he would feature me as the leading man. Poor little Hyacinth was to be a leading lady."

"That doesn't sound like anything that would get him murdered."

"He used people and then threw them away like garbage. His wife, for example." He spun her around. "Oh, she put a good face on it, but she knew he hadn't any feelings left for her, except indifference. And I strongly believe that indifference can light a fire. One that smolders for years and then: kablam! It bursts into flame."

And you would know all about that her type of flame, wouldn't you, Mr. Calloway?

"So you think his wife did it?"

His eyebrows shot up. "Not really. I was just illustrating my point. It could really have been anyone he mistreated. Hyacinth, Daphne, his children, why even me, I suppose."

"Tell me about Hyacinth," she requested.

"I hear she has a new man," he said. "I'm surprised she didn't bring him tonight. He was on the set a few times. Powerful specimen. Looks like he strangles bears for fun."

"You paint a vivid picture," Catherine said. "I don't suppose you write, do you?"

"I do, as a matter of fact. Imagine your figuring that out! Are you psychic or something?"

Catherine's surprise at the accuracy of her guess clearly amused him. "No. But I do teach literature," she said.

"I don't write anything highbrow. Detective stories. That's my game. I've even had some published."

"How marvelous," she said. "Do you use a pen name?"

"Vance Conrad," he said, pride beaming from his eyes.

"I'll keep my eye out for them," she said.

The dance ended, and he led her back to the table. Mr. Darcy had now engaged Lady Naomi in conversation, presumably convincing her to come on his program. Catherine decided to tackle Daphne, who had just walked off the floor with Buck.

"May I speak with you for a few minutes?" she asked.

The woman sighed. "I suppose so," she said.

"How is your father?"

"He is fine, I guess. We continue to stay with Buck. He enjoys the library there."

"Tell me," said Catherine, leaning closer so she could lower her voice. "Did Mr. Fields have any idea that his wife had a lover? Was he having her followed?"

The woman's eyebrows puckered. "Ruth? Followed? Why would he do that?"

"I thought perhaps he might be gathering evidence for a divorce," Catherine said. "He hired a detective."

To her surprise, Daphne smiled briefly. "The darling. He never told me." She put a hand over her heart.

"Do you suppose he might have something about it in his apartment? A report or something?"

Daphne bit her lower lip in thought. "Yes. That would be the place. It wouldn't do for that kind of thing to be in the studio or at his house."

"Do you have a key to the apartment? It might do a lot to clear things up if we could find a report."

"Of course," said Daphne. She opened the small clutch bag and took out a yale key on a silver key ring. "Don't forget to return it. I go there sometimes. Just to think."

"I also wanted to talk to you about your stalker. Is he still bothering you?" asked Catherine.

Daphne looked around furtively. "I haven't noticed him lately. Perhaps Buck has scared him off."

"Perhaps he killed the man you loved and then framed you for it. Maybe that is part of his game," Catherine said. She had only come up with this idea on the spur of the moment and realized too late how cruel she sounded.

Daphne's eyes filled with tears. "Yes. Did Buck tell you the man rang the police and told them he heard us quarreling?"

"I'm sorry," said Catherine. "I think it's more likely that whoever killed Michael did it because of who Michael was. I very much doubt that it had anything to do with you."

"Then why did the murderer use my gun?" asked Daphne, removing a handkerchief from her purse. She blotted her tears carefully. A slow, syrupy jazz tune played in the background, but she focused on the woman in front of her. *How much of what the actress said and did was acting, and how much was real?*

Catherine said, "Yes, you're right. You're right. Your gun is crucial. Did you always carry it in your purse? Even here in the club?"

"Yes," Daphne said. "I have thought of that. It had to have been taken either here or at the studio. And I didn't notice it was gone, so it must have been taken very close to the time of the murder."

Catherine concealed her elation. *Finally! Progress! That narrows the field of suspects down. It couldn't be the stalker because he wasn't at the club or the studio. That we know of.*

"Did Mrs. Fields ever join you here at the club or in the studio?"

Daphne took a very determined drink of her whiskey. "Very rarely. But she was at the studio the day before Michael was killed. I remember because she made a scene. I have no idea what prompted it, but I'm certain she has regretted it ever since."

Catherine wondered if the woman had known Daphne packed a gun in her purse.

"I assume you kept your purse in your dressing room?" she asked.

"Yes. The only people who would have had access to it were the other cast members who had dressing rooms down that hall. There is a guard there." She turned to greet Buck, who had brought her what looked like tonic water. "Thank you, darling. Why, this is tonic water!"

"Can't have you getting squiffy," he said gently. "Not with Richard Darcy around to make game of you."

"I just have one more question," Catherine asked, "Would Del Fields ever have had access to your gun?"

Daphne tilted her head and stared off. "The club isn't really his type of thing. But he did come to the set once while I was there. It was near the time of the murder, but I don't remember precisely when. Another scene. He and his father did not get along. It was a very contentious family."

"Darling," said Buck. "Surely that's enough for now? Let's dance."

The actress smiled, using all her star power. "Of course. If you'll excuse us, Catherine?"

Was Buck afraid of what she might say?

Harry came over. "Shall we dance?"

Once they were on the floor, he said, "Good conversation?"

"Wonderful. I've narrowed the list of suspects. I'll tell you once we've left here. Oh, and I've got the key to Fields' apartment office. And something occurred to me. Do you suppose Fields was having his wife followed because he suspected she was having an affair and wanted to use it as evidence in a divorce?"

"That thought had occurred to me. Jolly good work getting that key."

She wondered if they were getting close to the murderer. Catherine tried to shake off the feeling that everyone was watching her as she danced. Was Michael Fields' killer on the dance floor?

CHAPTER THIRTEEN

Richard Darcy's review of Harry's lecture on his morning show was fulsome with praise. He hinted that it was the slightest bit naughty and revealed that Harry would be reciting the iconic poems of the British War Poets the following Friday.

"What rubbish," said Harry, moving to turn off the wireless they had been listening to in the lounge.

"Oh, leave it on. I need to hear if he says anything about the murder."

In fact, he didn't mention the murder, but he reported on EPIC's coup in snagging the interest of the American president with its anti-poverty programs. Darcy drew quite a vivid picture of the meeting on Thursday night, mentioning the "lately murdered Michael Fields's son, Delano Fields—the up and coming young Communist." Catherine had no idea whether Del would be pleased or not.

Their day was full. This morning they were going to raid Fields' office. Then, assuming there was nothing that had to be followed up on urgently, they were going to drive the professor down to Laguna Beach, a small artist's colony Harry had heard about. They wanted to discuss Dr. Adler's impressions of those people he had met. He was still staying at Buck's, but Daphne and Buck would be on the movie set, even though it was Saturday.

They set out with high hopes for Michael Fields' apartment building which sat in a block near the MGM studio—unpretentious brick with a black entrance door. Catherine and Harry used Daphne's key and entered. They climbed up to the first floor, where they used the same key to open Apartment Number Three. There was no police tape sealing the entrance, fortunately.

When they entered, they found it was stifling and stale-smelling. Harry immediately opened all the windows and turned on the fans. The furnishings were modern Scandinavian—teak and glass. Covered with olive green fabric, the boxy couch looked uncomfortable. The floors were bare hardwood. Catherine doubted that Fields had entertained many visitors to this barren place.

The first room they tried was a bedroom. The bed was unmade, a blanket crumpled on the floor. A filing cabinet, desk, and typewriter occupied the next room.

Catherine went to the desk, Harry the filing cabinet.

"Locked," said Harry.

"Try this," Catherine handed him the small key she had found in the top desk drawer. There wasn't much else there other than pencils, paper clips, and a fountain pen.

She moved to the side drawers, which appeared to be filled with bank books and scripts. The bank book looked the most promising. Catherine started with the most recent check stub and worked her way back. Petty Cash/$100; Household/$250; Ruth/$150; Black/$150.

"There's a pretty hefty check here for Black in July. One Hundred Fifty Dollars. It seems to be a one-time occurrence. That must be the detective."

"Interesting," said Harry.

Catherine continued. In the earlier stubs, there was one each month to "D" for $300. The payments had stopped in July, but they went back to March, where they stopped.

"This is odd," she said. "Look." She held the bankbook up so Harry could see the stubs.

"Do you think "D" is for Del?" she asked.

"Most probably. But what would he need with $300 a month? That's a small fortune for a college student."

"Maybe it's for tuition and rent," said Catherine.

"Hmm. I'm still not satisfied. Let's keep that in mind. Here is my camera. Can you take some photos of those counterfoils while I finish with this file drawer? There's not much here."

Catherine took the photos.

"Ah! Here we are," said Harry. "A nice, fat manilla envelope labeled Ruth."

Opening it, he found all the evidence Field would ever have needed for a divorce naming Joe Calloway as the correspondent. Besides that, there's just some sort of dossier on someone he'd never heard of, some old phonebooks, and a bunch of ordinance survey maps of France.

When Catherine was finished with her photos, she handed the camera to Harry to photograph the drawer's contents. The other drawers were empty.

All in all, they were disappointed. "Maybe it will make sense later."

* * *

When they arrived at the neo-Georgian mansion, Ames, the butler, showed them through to the sunny sitting room.

"One thing about California," said Harry after they had greeted the professor. "The weather is always sunny! Haven't needed my brolly."

"It's far too hot for me," grumbled the professor.

"I think I'm finally getting used to the heat," Catherine told him. "We had the most fabulous time on Thursday afternoon. Our friend Max took us to the beach, and we swam in the ocean," said Catherine. "Have you been able to keep busy?"

"I am writing a monograph," the professor said. "It is quiet here during the day, and Buck has a comfortable study, though I don't believe he uses it much. It's a refuge for me to write about the psychological problems of people long dead."

"We saw your daughter last night at the Starlight Club. We made some good progress on our investigation," said Harry.

Professor Adler sighed, and Catherine noted the heaviness behind it. He was clearly disturbed.

"Dafna is still in mourning and will be for some time, I imagine. At least she is not in jail any longer. But the trial is only three weeks away."

Catherine said, "We're getting on. I think we've met everyone closest to Mr. Fields. It's too bad we don't have your impressions of them all. It would be a help. I agree with your daughter that the wife seems a likely suspect, but I can't think of any way that you could observe her so we could get your impressions."

"Perhaps you could tell me about your interview," the older man said. "What were your impressions of her?"

Catherine thought for a moment. "I think Mr. Fields designed the house with her in mind. It's stark and cold—all white. No colors. But she received us in her husband's study, which was all dark wood with Persian rugs and ruby upholstery. Quite the opposite."

The professor put the tips of his fingers together. "That is very telling, isn't it?"

"I thought so. Ruth is a pale blonde who looks like an English aristocrat. She thinks her husband was definitely having an affair with your daughter. She said she knew the look of a man in love," said Catherine.

"But she claimed she had her own lovers, so she wasn't jealous," said Harry. "And, we have evidence that that is true. Mr. Joseph Calloway, a cast member, picked her up and took her to his mansion, where they spent the whole afternoon together alone. We have photos of some evidence of their affair that we found in Michael Fields' office."

"Are you ready to go for a drive?" Catherine asked. "We can get you up to speed on the way. There is a beach south of here that sounds spectacular."

"That sounds lovely," said the professor.

When they were all settled in the car, with the professor sitting up front next to Harry, the professor resumed his questions.

"So she thinks Dafna did it? Did she give any reason?" asked the professor, his face set in lines of resignation.

"No. Although she also thought the murderer could be Buck," said Harry. "She said she didn't think Buck 'rang true.' What's your opinion of him?"

"I believe her judgment of Buck is very accurate, as a matter of fact. I have watched him closely. He is playing a role. But I think it's a role within a role," said the professor carefully.

Catherine leaned forward in her chair. "Do you know what the roles are?"

"First of all, I don't think he's an American. But he's also dreaming about being an upper-class Englishman. I don't think he's that either. You must have noticed that he has an accent that is neither American nor British. It's somewhere between the two."

"Yes!" said Catherine with some excitement. "Exactly!"

"Whoever he is," said the professor, "it's hidden well."

"What are his feelings for your daughter?" asked Harry, now leaning forward, as well.

"I have watched them when they are together. I believe he has a great but reserved love for her. When he is with her, he tries to cover up his feelings. But when she is talking to someone else— Lady Naomi, for instance—he watches her. I see the hunger in his eyes. It is clear."

Catherine looked out the window at the unlovely oil wells. "He is taking me to dinner tonight. I'm interested to know what's behind the invitation."

"You quite forgot to tell me about this, Catherine," said Harry. "I don't know that I am thrilled about your going out alone with a possible murderer."

"It's a fact-finding mission," she said. "Not a date."

"That doesn't make it any safer," Harry said with the stubborn look she knew hardening his square jaw.

"I shall make certain we go somewhere crowded if you like," she said. "You can follow us to and fro in the Chevrolet."

He released a sigh. "That will have to be satisfactory, I suppose." He looked at the professor, who appeared concerned. "Excuse us. I probably worry too much. Catherine has been attacked by murderers in the past."

"Oh, *Gott in Himmel*. I hope I have not put you in danger!"

"As you heard, we are taking precautions," said Harry. "Now back to your impressions of Buck. Do you think he could have murdered Fields out of jealousy?"

"When passion raises its head, as in this case," the older man said, "Anything is possible. One might say the same of fear."

This pronouncement made Catherine uncomfortable. As Harry had said, she was altogether too familiar with the truth of it.

She went on. "Joe Calloway, Ruth Fields' lover, is an interesting character, though I can't say I like him too much. He's the villain in the movie. We've had a couple of dances together, and he's managed to come across as a raging anti-Semite, as well as casting aspersions on Michael Fields's character. He had a good reason to kill Fields if he is in love with his wife. Ruth doesn't believe in divorce."

"He dislikes Dafna?"

"Yes. In fact, Calloway called L.A. a 'Jew town,'" Catherine said. "It was most unpleasant. I faked an ankle sprain to get away from him."

"I wonder what he meant by that," the professor said. She observed his profile as he looked out the window. To say it looked bleak was an understatement.

"Don't take it too personally, Professor," said Harry. "I've heard the same thing. I think there is a feeling that all the big producers, save only one, are Jewish. It's a kind of love-hate relationship. They've done a tremendous amount of good for the city by bringing the industry here, but I don't get the idea that they've ever really been accepted in their private personas."

The professor said, "They hate us if we're poor, but they hate us even more if we're successful."

Catherine felt confined in the car, where she could not pace her feelings out. She didn't like hearing this about people. It made her dashed uncomfortable. Especially, telling Professor Adler about it. Then she thought of what Del had told her.

"Mr. Fields's son is a rather enthusiastic Communist. He says there's another dangerous element that's come to town."

She told the professor about the Nazi, Helmut Grossman, and his plans for an "Aryan Western."

"I wonder if young Fields would have become a Communist if his father hadn't forbidden it," said the professor. "Did you have the feeling that he had something against his father?"

Harry said, "He is a true Utopian, I think. I'm not sure what path he traveled to get there. You could be right. Neither he nor his mother has an alibi for the murder, it turns out. And Del has a significant financial motive. His father has cut him off."

"Interesting." said the professor.

"You never said if you got anything more out of that sourpuss Calloway when you danced with him last night. We got sidetracked."

Catherine sat back on the window seat and crossed her legs. "He didn't like the murdered man much. Said he used the people in his life and then threw them away 'like garbage.' He included Daphne in the list."

"It doesn't take a psychologist to see that Calloway is one bitter man," said Harry. "I haven't heard the director that roundly denounced before. I wonder if he's right or just bitter. Though one would think his affair with the man's wife would assuage some of the bitterness."

"I'll ask my daughter when we are private," said Professor Adler. "It could be important. Or it could, as you say, be the opinion of a bitter man."

Catherine didn't hold out much hope of Daphne confirming such an accusation to her father. If she had been used, her father was probably the last person she would tell.

Chapter Fourteen

Laguna Beach was indeed picturesque atop cliffs overlooking the sea. Catherine sat on the sand, watching the waves crash against a rock promontory extending out into the ocean. It reminded her greatly of Cornwall. It was restful and conducive to thought.

She thought of her parents with whom she was newly reconciled and wondered about her father's health. He had suffered a brutal heart attack in January. Her brother, Wills, was checking on them from time to time but would soon be leaving for Africa to oversee his waterworks project in Kenya.

She suddenly felt very cut off from her life in England. It all seemed so distant from this place where the sun was always shining, and everything was so new. So many things seemed like a false front—a stage set.

Restless, she got up and walked down to the sea. Carrying her shoes in her hand, she let the water wash over her toes. This place was elemental, however. Original. Right here on this beach, she could imagine the essential California before it had been beset by oil wells, movie people, and property developers.

Would they ever find the answer to this crazy case full of pretend people? She didn't feel like she really knew any of them, least of all Daphne. It would break her father's heart if she were guilty and had to suffer the death penalty. He would probably never recover from it.

And what about Buck? Why this dinner? What did he want from her?

Liking how the sea breeze was gently blowing away the heat, Catherine decided to walk over the rocky promontory to the next cove. She held her sunhat to her head and picked her way through the rugged formations beneath her feet. She reached the next beach with relief. She wasn't wearing the right shoes for this.

As she walked along the edge of the water, she saw another couple coming toward her. They were dressed in bathing costumes, and her eyes at once riveted themselves on the man. What a build! He was brown from the sun, his hair blond, and it seemed to her that his muscles had muscles.

"Catherine!" the petite woman called. She realized it was Hyacinth who was holding hands with the Greek god. Her bathing costume was very brief, showing her lovely figure to advantage.

"Hyacinth!" Catherine called. "Fancy!"

Drawing level with them, she saw the actress looked smug.

"Have you met Helmut?" Hyacinth asked.

"I haven't had the pleasure," Catherine answered.

The man held out his large, square hand to shake hers. His grip was firm. "Helmut Grossman," he said. The light blue eyes looking her over were startling in his tanned face.

"Catherine Tregowyn," she said. "How do you do?" She had heard the man's name, but for the moment, she couldn't think where. His towering presence was rather disconcerting.

"This is my favorite beach," Hyacinth said. "Michael used to bring me here. I like all the little coves. So much more private than the bigger beaches like Santa Monica and Huntington."

"Unfortunately, I'm not dressed for bathing," Catherine said. "How is the water?"

"Warm as bathwater!" said Hyacinth. "We've been swimming ages."

"You are British," the man said. "Are you an actress, too?"

"No. I teach at the university," Catherine said. "I met Hyacinth at the Starlight Club."

"She is a friend of Buck's," said the woman. "But are you here all alone?"

"No. Harry and Daphne's father are walking along the cliffs. I prefer the beach."

"Shall we sit for a moment?" asked Mr. Grossman. He walked away from the surf a bit and unfolded the towel he carried under his arm.

"How kind," murmured Catherine. Watching his precise movements as he spread the towel on the sand, she suddenly realized where she had heard his name. He was the Nazi director that Del Fields had told them about at lunch. The one who was making the "Aryan Western."

"What is your interest in Hollywood?" Catherine asked the man.

"I am making a film. A Western."

"But how fascinating! We Europeans are enthralled by Westerns," Catherine told him.

He asked her what her subject was. She told him and said, "You must be a student of American history if you have written a film about it."

"Helmut is brilliant," said Hyacinth. "He sees our history as an epic struggle."

Catherine said nothing but could hardly agree. *An epic struggle between cannons on the one side and bows and arrows on the other side?*

At that moment, she heard a hello shouted from atop the cliff. Turning, she saw Harry waving. Suddenly, she thought it might not be a good idea for the professor and Mr. Grossman to have an encounter. If the rumors of him being a Nazi were true.

"Stay where you are! I'm coming up," she called. Turning to Hyacinth and her companion, she said. "I'm afraid I must go. I have a dinner engagement back in Los Angeles. It was lovely to meet you, Mr. Grossman. Good luck with your film."

* * *

"Did you make some new friends?" asked Harry when they were in the car headed for L.A.

"That was Hyacinth," said Catherine. "And you'll never guess who she was with, and acting very chummy, I might add."

"Who?"

"The director Del was so worked up about," she said. "He called him a Nazi. Helmut Grossman!"

"A Nazi?" said the professor. "Here in Laguna Beach?"

"He's going to make a film with Daryl Zanuck. A Western," she said. "I don't think he is any threat to you, Herr Doktor."

"I wonder if there are any female roles in it to fill," said Harry.

Catherine laughed. "My thoughts exactly. Hyacinth was treating him rather like her prize bull. I must say, he does have a fine physique."

The professor made a sound that sounded like "phtt."

Harry gave her a stern look and said, "The professor was telling me about some California history while we were walking. There was a Spanish priest in the Eighteenth Century, Father Serra, who walked the state and established missions all the way up the coast. The first towns in California grew around the missions."

"There are a few history books in Mr. Danforth's library," explained the professor.

"Hmm," said Catherine. "Mr. Calloway mentioned Father Serra. I had no idea who he was talking about. Those missions might be interesting to visit sometime. Something genuinely old."

* * *

Catherine dressed in her all-purpose black frock for her evening with Buck. She never could have imagined when she was packing in Oxford how warm it was going to be. She was glad she had researched it and packed some lightweight evening wear.

Buck was very complimentary when he saw her. He led her to his Rolls which he was driving himself this evening.

"Where are we going?" she asked.

"Do you like seafood?"

"I do," Catherine replied.

"I thought we might go down to Santa Monica to a little restaurant that serves delicious fish and crab."

"That sounds good to me."

"What have you been doing today? You look like you've had some sun."

"We drove down to Laguna Beach. It's lovely down there."

They spoke of the places she and Harry had seen and her impressions of California as being so new.

"Have you ever been to Europe?" she asked him.

"I've visited London," he said. "Here we are, then. I hope you brought your appetite."

The place they were to eat was small, tucked away from the boulevard on a little side street. Catherine could smell the aroma of seafood before they had even gone inside.

As Buck helped her out of his car, Catherine glanced behind her to see the Chevrolet with Harry at the wheel. This wasn't exactly the large, crowded restaurant she had promised him, but maybe a small, crowded restaurant would be sufficiently public.

Buck continued to be courteous as he pulled out her chair at the table which he had reserved. He was acting oddly purposeful, as though he were a man with a mission he didn't particularly relish.

The restaurant was clearly a favorite with the locals and not decorated with upper crust tourists in mind. Catherine felt a bit conspicuous in her cocktail dress. Draped in red checked oilcloth, the tables each had an oil lantern at the center. Fishing nets, from which dried starfish depended, draped the walls.

"What is the best thing to eat here?" she asked as she looked over the menu.

"Definitely the crab, but if you would rather not have shellfish, any of the grilled fish is good. I find grilling preserves the taste far better than frying or baking," Buck advised her.

"Is Red Snapper good?" she asked.

"Excellent. And local. If you like fish, you would like it. If you're not a big fish fan, any of the creamed dishes will appeal to you more."

"No. I believe I'll have the Snapper. I'm quite used to fish. I grew up in Cornwall. I used to go fishing with my brother," Catherine told him.

"You look far too glamorous. I can't imagine you with a fishing rod."

Catherine laughed. "My brother and his friend, Rafe, were my favorite companions when I was growing up. The Three Musketeers." She must be nervous. She was chattering.

Buck smiled absently at this information and gave the waitress their order. He ordered beer for himself and inquired of Catherine what she would like to drink.

"I'll have a lemonade," she said after consulting the menu again.

Buck relaxed back in his chair and unfolded his napkin. Placing it on his lap, he said, "How goes your mission to help Daphne?"

Catherine hadn't expected the question. Though it was couched in casual tones, Buck's eyes were intense.

"We're still gathering facts," she said. "So far, there aren't any favorites. We even have a Communist."

He raised his hand and stroked the hair on the back of his head. "You know I care for Daphne?"

"Yes."

Buck continued, "What you don't know is this town. Not so long ago, it was part of the Wild West. Hollywood has a veneer of sophistication, but it's only a veneer." He paused and leaned forward on his elbows. "Everyone who calls himself an actor wants fame and fortune. The posing, the gossip, the verbal back-stabbing--they're all part of it. Actors are always playing a part."

"I think I've begun to realize that," Catherine said. In fact, she wondered what part Buck was acting now. Or was this slightly menacing personality his authentic self?

"Good. It's hard for someone new to our town to avoid stepping on toes."

"It sounds like you're trying to warn me. But I don't want to be a successful actress. I just want to see justice done."

"What I'm telling you is that you're bound to ruffle feathers, and you may even get hurt. If Daphne didn't kill Fields, that means someone else did. And they're not going to be all British and civilized about it. You're in danger from that person."

Catherine didn't know how to reply to this.

"And do you realize what a hornet's nest you could possibly stir up in the Communist community by pursuing Del as a suspect? They are even more gloves-off than actors. When it comes to protecting one of their own, they don't play like gentlemen."

He was making her angry. "Thanks for the warning, but are you trying to tell me that I should leave Daphne's fate to the police who have already arrested her for murder?"

"Why is it that you're so certain she's innocent?"

Catherine was astounded. Wasn't this man in love with Daphne?

The waitress brought their order, but she had completely lost her appetite. Not so, Buck. He fell to pulling apart and cracking the crab before him. His enthusiasm for the task repulsed her. However, she did notice that when he used utensils, he held them like a European.

"Don't you think she's innocent?" asked Catherine

"It's not important to me whether she is or not. I'm under the woman's spell, for better or for worse, I'm afraid." He said the words with an intensity enhanced by the violent way he dismembered the crab. It made her feel a bit ill.

"Well, her father thinks her incapable of murder. That's what I'm banking on," said Catherine. She ate a forkful of rice, but she might as well have been chewing moldy bread.

He gave a wry chuckle. "Oh, she's capable all right. Her mother was Russian, you know. Daphne's all passion, through and through." He looked at her keenly. "You didn't know that, did you?"

"But why would she kill the man she loved?" Catherine was growing increasingly uncomfortable. She lowered her eyes to her plate.

He laughed. "I'm glad to see you bought that. It was a masterful performance."

Daphne's elaborate confession of love for Michael Fields had all been an act? Why? If it was, it must have been for her and Harry's benefit. Some sort of subterfuge. Was Daphne guilty then? Or was she covering for Buck, whom she really loved? Was Buck himself the murderer?

"Are you always so gullible?" he asked. "I wouldn't have thought it of a suave, sophisticated intellectual like you."

That stung. "I'm actually reckoned a good judge of character. I dislike being manipulated," she said. "Why would she want Harry and me to think she had a secret passion for Fields?"

"Because she thinks it makes her more sympathetic. She was playing up to you."

Catherine didn't buy that explanation. If it had been an act, it had been an elaborate one. Maybe she convinced Buck it was all for show, but Catherine wasn't ready to settle on one version of Daphne or the other. The woman was even more complex than she had imagined. Her father had seemed to believe Daphne had been in love with Fields and that Buck's love was possibly unrequited. Maybe the actress liked to have as many men as possible in her thrall.

Buck put out a hand and grabbed her arm, his look determined. Her arm hurt. There was a menace in his grip.

"I'm sorry, but Daphne takes people in all the time. Part of her charm is that you never know the truth. But the fact is, that guilty or no, I care for her damnably. I am raising hell to try to get the arrest charge dropped. I've got detectives; I'm even trying bribes. I'm afraid that what you and Bascombe are doing is going to get in my way. You see, I don't care who murdered Fields. I just don't want Daph to suffer for it."

Catherine wrenched her arm away. Harry must have witnessed Buck's grip on her arm, for he had managed his way through the tables and was at her side.

"Hands to yourself, mate," he said.

Before standing up, Catherine said, "You've managed to leave your sense of British Fair Play behind in your native country, Mr. Danforth. Or maybe you never had it, and it caused a stir. Is that why you left? I can quite see you as a bully boy."

He started as though he had been burned.

That's punctured your facade. I've nailed you spot on.

Buck Danforth's eyes narrowed, and his whole face took on the look of a first-class villain.

She and Harry left.

"What happened? Did he threaten you?"

"In a way. I'll tell you all about it in the car. Sorry about your dinner."

* * *

When Harry had heard Catherine's summary of her very strange conversation, he said, "I'm glad I followed you with the car. The charm he's noted for seems to have slipped. It's a long way back to Westwood on foot."

Once they were back at the Inn, Harry and Catherine sought a more congenial dinner at the local diner. They managed to get a somewhat quiet booth away from the counter. Catherine's thoughts were in such a whirl, her appetite was still in upheaval. She just ordered chicken noodle soup.

"Astounding," said Harry. "Do you really believe Daphne was acting when she proclaimed her love for Michael Fields?"

"Buck certainly believes it. But then Daphne could have been acting when she told him she was acting, couldn't she?"

"That conversation is capable of a lot of interpretations," Harry said. "I wonder if he really thinks Daphne guilty? What do you think?"

Their food was delivered, and Catherine was glad of something warm but light and nourishing to settle her.

"He says he doesn't know or care if she is guilty," Catherine said. "He is just trying to get her off. Apparently, the police are susceptible to bribes. He's not interested in the truth. What worries him is that that might be *our* motivation. You heard me accuse him of being a Brit who has lost his sense of fair play. I couldn't help it. But now he knows that *we* are operating on that basis. He's afraid that our work is going to collide with his. He was trying to bully me."

"I know that the professor has believed in his daughter from the beginning. I know that he still believes in her. But is he aware of what Buck is doing? If so, does he approve? Or does Adler see us as a danger, too?" Harry wondered aloud.

Catherine was aware of a low rumble in her nervous system. Her feet wouldn't be still, and her hands were trembling. She pulled herself together. "You know, I'm past caring," said Catherine. "Buck's warning to me backfired. I hold Professor Adler in great esteem, but even if he doesn't want us to proceed, I will. I want to get at the truth of this."

"I know. It's very strange. Buck's warning has made me determined to get to the bottom of this, too." said Harry. "But I have a feeling we are up against something we don't understand. Buck's right about that. It's never struck me as strange, but why is the studio really paying for Daphne's defense? What should we know about MGM? And how do we find out?"

Catherine thought as she pulled apart and buttered her roll. "You know, much as I hate to suggest it, maybe our best source for something like this would be Richard Darcy. If anyone has the pulse of the movie studios, it would be him. At any rate, it will be a good excuse to get the gossip about the cast."

"You're right. And the other night after my lecture, he gave me his card in case I changed my mind about appearing on his show," said Harry. "It has his home line on it. I suppose gossip doesn't sleep. I can ring him in the morning."

"Good idea," said Catherine. She had had another idea that she didn't like very much.

"Do you suppose you could ring Lady Naomi at the Beverly Wilshire Hotel tomorrow morning and see if she'd fancy spending some time with you? She might have some observations about Daphne and life at *Chez Danforth*."

"Are you throwing me into the lion's den, then? Who knows where that will lead?" asked Harry.

"I'll be sitting close by behind a plant or something. You may be the one who requires rescuing in this case." She gripped her hands in her lap. "It's absurd that I'm still shaking. Thank you so much for insisting on being close at hand."

"I wasn't sure which way he was going to jump," said Harry. "Maybe I sensed that he was a phony."

"He's worse than a phony." She looked down at her arm where Buck had grasped it. "Look. He left a bruise on my arm."

"The blighter! He wants punching. I say, Catherine, I'm more than ready to get this thing solved. Let's be off and act like good little Communists at our ANL meeting."

* * *

The Anti-Nazi League meeting was much like the EPIC meeting—people milling about the meeting room in fashionable clothes, talking as though they were at a cocktail party. They were quick to see Del standing amid youths who looked like university students.

Daphne was also there, accompanied by Professor Adler. Harry and Catherine approached them.

"What are you doing here?" asked Daphne. "You think Michael was murdered by an ANL member?"

"Stranger things have happened," said Catherine. "What can you tell us about Del Fields? He has an extensive inheritance, I should think."

"He's a hothead," said Daphne. "He was continually fighting with his father over his politics. Michael was convinced this was just a phase."

"It is strange that he is now wealthy," said the professor.

"Yes," said Daphne, shaking her head. "It will be interesting to see what he does with the money. And his Papa is no longer available to get him out of trouble." The actress surveyed the people in the room. "I joined this chapter because I wanted to be involved, but it isn't like the one in Paris. These people are planning something big. Something like the Stock Exchange Bombing, I think," said Daphne.

A gavel sounded, and the talking died down.

A husky-looking man said, "Ladies and Gentlemen, tonight we meet because we are facing a threat. Action is required. Here to tell us about it is Delano Fields."

Michael Fields' son stood at the portable podium. He gave the same speech about Helmut Grossman to the assembled audience that he gave to Catherine and Harry. Then he added, "Daryl Zanuck has decided to produce this movie. It is time for us to act."

He turned the podium back over to Mr. Husky.

"We will start picketing the studio tomorrow. We will also picket the Zanuck productions that are now being shown in the theaters, asking for a boycott. I have a mimeographed list here. Be sure to pick one up before you leave. The picket signs have all been printed. Do not take one unless you plan to use it. They weren't cheap to produce. They are in the next room.

"This action is the most important one we have taken yet. We need to change Zanuck's mind now!"

There was loud applause. The audience crowded into the room next door to get its picket signs. The mimeograph sheets of current Zanuck productions disappeared quickly.

"Phew!" said Catherine. "I wouldn't want to be Daryl Zanuck.

She and Harry had been deserted by the Adlers and found themselves amidst such an enthusiastic crowd that it took time for them to reach the library exit.

"That was really quite something," said Harry.

* * *

It was difficult for Catherine to let Harry go that night. He kissed her with unwonted fervor at the door to her room. She found herself clinging to him after their kiss. She'd always detested clinging women.

"How much longer is it going to take before you decide to marry me?" he asked.

"Harry, darling, you've been so patient with me. Can you keep it up a bit longer? I think being in America is helping me to let go of the past and the fool I was for all those years. And one by one, you are sweeping away all my doubts about myself. I've been thinking you're rather like a tidal wave."

"Prepare to be swept away," he said, kissing her again.

Chapter Fifteen

Richard Darcy agreed to meet them for brunch at the Beverly Wilshire. They had a date afterward with Lady Naomi. Catherine dressed a bit daringly in a pair of navy linen trousers and a red and white polka-dot silk blouse. She wore her cartwheel hat.

Harry met her in the lounge, and she kissed him good morning with a new eagerness. Sitting close to him on the Chevrolet's bench seat, she enjoyed the crystal clear morning and even the climbing temperature. It was going to be hard to reacclimate herself to English weather when she went home at the end of the month.

Mr. Darcy was outfitted in white linen with a Panama hat. Effusive in his welcome, he led them to a table on the Boulevard Restaurant terrace overlooking the swimming pool. He claimed it was saved for him each Sunday morning. When they were seated, the waiter handed them menus and said there was also a brunch buffet inside with custom-made omelets available.

Catherine could never resist a good omelet and chose the buffet. Harry did likewise. The men had daiquiris and Catherine fresh orange juice. The food was lovely, and so was the setting.

When all the niceties had been performed, Harry said, "As visitors to Hollywood, we thought we would take advantage of your vast knowledge of how things operate here. We have become curious about the big studios like MGM. What's their history? How do they operate?"

"Yes," said Mr. Darcy. "We do have a rather unique situation here, don't we? As a matter of fact, our movie moguls are mostly Jews who have relocated from New York. They built their fortunes during the silent film era and have led the way in the motion picture business ever since."

He paused to sip his daiquiri. Before him was a huge plate of pancakes, shirred eggs, ham, and fruit salad.

"You mention MGM," he continued. "I am a close friend of Louis Mayer. He is unusual in that he is very conservative politically. Most of these fellows like Jack Warner, for instance, have very liberal politics." He speared a mouthful of pancakes.

"But Mayer has always tried to fit in with the WASP's—white Anglo-Saxon Protestants—so he prizes family values. He was hand-in-glove with President Hoover and did lots newsreels featuring happy hearths and homes to try to pacify the public after the stock market crash."

He gave a little laugh. "Unfortunately, he backed the wrong horse. FDR isn't interested in that sort of thing. He cares more about the future."

"How fascinating!" said Catherine. "We understand he paid the bail for Miss Binoche and has hired her defense counsel. Is that the kind of thing he does?"

"His studio is family to him. He has a special relationship with Daphne. Michael brought her over from Paris, you know." Even though he had been talking non-stop, the broadcaster had put away the whole of his pancakes.

"Louis watches the European films in his own private home theater and is always on the lookout for new talent," he said. "He was thrilled to sign Miss Binoche. She is like a daughter to him. You know she is also Jewish. Hopefully, she will be cleared of this murder, and his confidence in her will be justified."

"What a fascinating relationship," said Catherine, who had

vastly enjoyed her omelet. "I am interested in the other moguls. Are they also Jewish?"

"All but one. And they are politically in a completely different camp than Louis. Because of the goings-on in Europe, many of the moguls and their stars are Anti-Nazi. To that end, some of them have joined the Communist Party. Secretly, but one finds out these things."

"Let me guess. Daryl Zanuck's studio is the only non-Jewish studio."

"As a matter of fact, you're right. Any particular reason you say that?"

"According to the Anti-Nazi League, he's agreed to produce a Fascist film.

Harry related their experience at the ANL the night before.

"That doesn't surprise me at all, but it's bad news for Zanuck," said the radio host.

"Del Fields was there," Harry remarked. Catherine watched Darcy's face. "He was certainly worked up."

"Yes. To the despair of his late father, Del is unashamedly Communist," Darcy said. " He was disowned by him lately."

Catherine thought of the check stubs. The payments to "D" had stopped last month.

"How well do you know Del?" she asked.

"Reasonably well, as a matter of fact. He has appeared on my show before, calling for support of EPIC. Politics is his life, and I like a bit of controversy in my programs. Keeps the ratings up."

Catherine was enjoying this seemingly vast font of information. "How long have you been in radio?" she asked.

She had an immediate impression of annoyance, but it was like a photographer's flash—gone in an instant.

"I've been doing my show for three years."

Harry said, "I can't believe it's only been three years. You sound like a veteran broadcaster. How does one go about becoming the font of all knowledge?"

"Gossip, you mean?" he laughed. "I started out with my

column. There's nothing more fun than gathering dirt. It's child's play. But, I hope I've grown up a little. Become more sophisticated."

Mopping up the syrup with his toast, he continued, "I've known the Fields all during that time. Ruth Delano Fields is not a woman you want to cross, believe me." He stabbed the air with his fork. "She has connections. She is old money, and that counts for something in this town of *nouveau riches*. Everyone's from somewhere else, and a lot of them just got here."

"Speaking of which," said Catherine. "We're British. You're not. Why the phony accent?"

Darcy laughed. "Adds a bit of authenticity to what I say. My Jersey accent makes me sound like a thug. But I wouldn't go around questioning people's accents if I were you."

"Are you trying to warn us?" asked Harry.

"Word gets around fast in this town. And I hear everything. I understand you're working on getting Daphne Binoche off."

"Actually, we've changed our focus," said Harry. "Now we're just looking for the truth of what happened."

Mr. Darcy pushed away his empty plate. "But you are professors. Foreigners. Why? And how far do you think you're going to get?"

"We started out trying to help Daphne's father. He is undone over all this. We've had a little experience with this sort of thing before," Harry said.

"We think the truth is in everyone's interest, except the guilty person," said Catherine. "I've been threatened, and I don't like it."

When did I become so stubborn? There is something about the people here that brings it out in me.

"Who threatened you?" asked Mr. Darcy.

"I think I'll keep that to myself," said Catherine.

"Well, I don't think Daphne is guilty, as a matter of fact," said Richard Darcy, interlacing his fingers across his ample middle. "But I haven't any idea who killed Michael. All I know is this place can be crazy. Gun laws aren't what you're used to in Britain. Just about anyone can own a gun. And we don't have the equivalent of the village constable going around to make sure the peace is kept. Plus, these people, these actors, they're pretty emotional people. It doesn't do to upset them."

"We'll be careful," said Harry. "We've been up against some pretty desperate criminals before."

The radio show host laughed. "You make a practice of this?"

"We've found ourselves in the middle of more than one murder case," said Catherine.

"But not in America," Mr. Darcy said. "I just ask you to bear in mind that things are different here. The police are of a different class. And then there's the District Attorneys. They're not like the King's Counsel. They're a nasty bunch . . ."

Catherine was irritated. "While we greatly appreciate your concern, we weren't born yesterday," she said. "I think we can manage." Suddenly, she smiled. "But we always have you to explain to us how things work in America."

He patted her hand. "Of course. I'll be glad to be your consultant. Someone has to keep you from bumbling into a hornet's nest." He finished off his daiquiri. "Listen, I've got to go now, but let's get together again. There are things you should know."

"Thanks," said Harry. "That would be helpful. Just give us a call when you can fit us into your schedule. With morning and evening broadcasts, you must be really busy."

"You've been marvelous," said Catherine.

The man preened himself. "Always happy to oblige a beautiful woman," he said.

* * *

At Catherine's request, Harry had extended an invitation to Lady Naomi to accompany them to see San Gabriel mission that afternoon. As they awaited her in the hotel lobby, Catherine finally asked the question that had been bothering her since their first encounter with the woman on the Queen Mary.

"Are you ever going to tell me about your past with the lady?"

"Who? You mean Lady Naomi?"

Catherine could tell he was stalling while he ordered his thoughts and decided what to say to her.

"Let's just say our relationship was fraught with class conflict. I should have known better than to get involved with a Marquess's daughter," Harry said finally.

"Well, whatever the problem, it doesn't seem to have affected her feelings for you," said Catherine.

"I sincerely doubt that Lady Naomi has feelings like a normal person."

Catherine was startled by the bitterness in his voice.

"I'm sorry," she said. "I can tell I've recalled a sore subject."

"You deserve to know," he said. "But it's all long ago. Back when she and I were undergraduates."

"You were in love with her?" asked Catherine, bracing herself for the answer.

"If you can believe it," Harry said, his jaw tight, "I was blind to her narcissism. I thought her frightfully exotic."

He stood up from the barrel chair where he had been sitting and walked away from her. She saw him square his shoulders as though preparing to go on, but at that moment, the subject of their conversation joined them.

"There's been another murder!" she announced to Harry, ignoring Catherine. "Downtown. By the library. I heard it at Buck's house on the wireless."

"How bizarre!" said Catherine. "Who was killed?"

Lady Naomi stayed focused on Harry but said, "A German called Helmut Grossman. Buck and Daphne think it could be good news for her. Two murders in Hollywood? How could they not be connected?"

"Heavens," said Catherine. "Tell her, Harry. Tell her about the meeting last night."

Harry obliged, and the lady was stunned. "Daphne and her father were at that meeting!"

"Yes," said Catherine. "Did they say when the murder occurred?"

"The body was discovered at 10:30 p.m., they said. What time did the meeting break up?" asked Lady Naomi.

"Right about then," said Catherine. "And it was one frenzied crowd. Did they say how he was killed?"

"Gunshot," said the lady. "But there was no weapon at the scene."

Lady Naomi said, "Daphne said he writes . . . wrote his own scripts," she went on. "He tried to convince Michael to direct it. But Michael said Louis would never go for it. She didn't say why, but the fact is, they knew each other. He hasn't been in the States long. Only about six months." She gave a theatrical shiver. "There are entirely too many shootings around here to suit me. I'm thinking of leaving for home."

"What about your screen test?" Catherine couldn't help asking. They moved to a small grouping of upholstered chairs in the corner of the hotel lobby.

The other woman finally looked at her. "That's been held up. But I don't have much faith in the new director—John Hale. He's still finding his feet. It's not like having a good screen test with Michael."

Catherine said, "I hope poor Hyacinth didn't hear it on the wireless."

"What does Hy have to do with anything?" asked Lady Naomi.

"They were going about together," said Catherine. "I saw them just yesterday afternoon in Laguna Beach."

"I've been to her flat," said Lady Naomi. "I wonder if we should go see her."

Catherine thought this over. "Is it far from here?" she asked.

"It's less than a mile away," Lady Naomi answered.

Catherine rose and looked out at the boulevard, but she didn't see the cars whizzing by. Instead, she was remembering the happy light in Hyacinth's eyes the day before. "Maybe you and I should go," she said. "I don't think she'd want Harry witnessing her distress."

"That's all right," said Harry. "I'll amuse myself with the Sunday Crossword. I'll meet you back here."

* * *

In the taxi, Lady Naomi said, "You're a baron's daughter if I'm not mistaken. Have you met Harry's parents yet?"

"As a matter of fact, no," said Catherine in surprise.

"Common," she said. "Utterly common. And they treated me like Harry's bit of stuff."

Catherine suppressed a grin. Not knowing what to say, she refrained from answering.

Hyacinth lived in a modern building of sandstone with an Art Deco entrance. Lady Naomi led the way inside to the lift. They traveled up four flights.

The actress answered the door, dressed in a blue satin dressing gown. Knowing instinctively that Hyacinth hadn't heard the news, Catherine said, "May we come in? I'm afraid we have bad news."

"The show has been canceled?" The young woman's eyes darted from one of her guests to the other. Then she pulled the door wide.

The flat was in wild disorder discarded clothing or dishes on nearly every surface. Cigarette smoke hung in the air.

Lady Naomi said, "I guess you haven't listened to the news."

"No. I can't abide the radio unless it's playing music. What has happened?"

Catherine took a deep breath. "Mr. Grossman has been killed. Shot," she said.

Hyacinth immediately lost her color and then fainted where she stood.

Kneeling next to the actress, Catherine chaffed her hand for a moment until Hyacinth's blue eyes opened. She stared into Catherine's face. "Tell me it isn't true," she said.

"I'm afraid it is," Catherine said gently.

"When did it happen?"

"Last night. About 10:30."

Hyacinth struggled to sit and then rubbed her eyes. "He was meeting someone about then."

"Do you know who it was?"

The actress struggled to her feet and immediately went to her cigarettes on the coffee table. She lit one with shaking hands. "He wouldn't give me a name. It was his blackmailer. He only told me that he was going to nail him to the wall."

Her voice was passionless. Catherine suspected shock.

Lady Naomi asked, "He was going to kill him?"

"No," The actress collapsed on her sofa and took a long drag on her cigarette. "He had information. It would have killed the guy's career. Helmut said the blackmailer would have been finished."

"So he was blackmailing him back?" Lady Naomi said.

"Yeah. Helmut was no dummy. Pretty smart, huh?" Hyacinth said.

"So smart it got him killed," said Lady Naomi.

"Did he tell you what he found out about the blackmailer?" asked Catherine.

"All I know was that the guy was dirty. Helmut didn't want me involved."

Catherine's thoughts immediately flew to Michael Fields' murder. Did the German know the murderer?

"Hyacinth, you need to call the police," Catherine said.

"No," the actress said. "There's no way I'm going to let Helmut's killer think that someone out there knows what Grossman knew. It could backfire on me. I want to stay alive, thank you."

Lady Naomi surprised Catherine by agreeing with Hyacinth. "You have to think of your own safety first."

Hyacinth suddenly sagged against the sofa. "I guess there's no way Helmut's film will be made now."

Catherine asked, "Was he giving you a part in it?"

"Yeah. The female lead."

"That's rotten," said Lady Naomi.

* * *

Harry was waiting for them when they returned to the Beverly Wilshire. Catherine and Lady Naomi alternated telling him what they had learned.

"Well, that is jolly interesting," he said. "But not for Grossman. It's odd that he was shot right next to the ANL meeting."

"What's the ANL?" asked Lady Naomi.

Harry explained, adding a summary of the night's business.

"They have something here in the West they call 'vigilante justice'--taking the law into your own hands," said Lady Naomi. "It could have been anyone in that group."

"I especially worry about Del," Catherine said. "He's got a guilty secret. He could have blackmailed Helmut Grossman about any number of things he might not have wanted to come to light. I suspect Grossman was connected to all the Nazi leaders."

Harry said, "I don't know about that. I think if Del had something on him, he would have told everyone about it—painting him as black as possible. I don't think he would have blackmailed him."

Catherine thought about this. "On second thought, I believe you're right about that. He doesn't work as a blackmailer. But what about Michael Fields' murderer? He could be the blackmailer."

"There is that, of course," said Harry. "Or Daphne's stalker. Either of them would have been desperate not to be known."

"Who do you two think you are? Tommy and Tuppence?" asked Lady Naomi.

Harry ignored her and said, "Perhaps we had better give Dr. Adler a ring. Who knows how he is taking this?"

"He was a little shaken this morning when we heard the news," said Lady Naomi. "Are you his minder or something?"

"Something," said Harry curtly. "I'm afraid this puts to rest our afternoon plans. Sorry, Nay."

"Oh, that's all right. I rather fancy a horseback ride. I've got the address of some stables in Pasadena that rent out mounts for riding in the foothills. I'm off."

They parted with the intrepid woman. She went off to find her stables, and Catherine used the lobby telephone to ring Buck's residence.

When the professor came to the telephone, he said, "I have been trying to reach you. Thank you so much for calling. The police are on their way. They have just identified Dafna's stalker. It seems it was Helmut Grossman."

Chapter Sixteen

Catherine's heart pounded. "Crikey," she said. "We'll be right over, Herr Professor."

But before they left the Beverly Wilshire, she decided to call Richard Darcy to see if he had any more details on the Grossman murder.

"I can only talk for a few minutes," the radio host told her. "I'm getting ready for a special broadcast tonight, but I have a few details for you."

He told Catherine that the victim had been an intimate of William Randolph Hearst, the conservative newspaper billionaire. Earlier in his life, he had met the director Leni Riefenstahl at a Hitler rally in Nuremberg and had collaborated with her in the making of the classic Nazi film, *Triumph of the Will*.

Grossman himself was to have played the larger-than-life hero in his movie with Zanuck, seeing himself as the perfect specimen of Aryan manhood. The plot would have involved an iconic battle between the Aryans and the Indians, who apparently figured into Grossman's idea of a sub-species.

Evidently, the gossip broadcaster had not uncovered the information about Grossman approaching Michael Fields first with his movie. When Catherine completed her report to Harry of her conversation, Harry brought up this fact.

"Could Grossman have murdered Fields?" she wondered aloud. "No, that's insane. According to Del, it was Louis Mayer who turned down his script, not Del's father."

"Still, it's interesting that they have a connection," said Harry.

"Yes," mused Catherine. "But then Hollywood is remarkably like a village in many ways."

As they drove to Buck's house, Catherine said, "I'm happy that Daphne won't have to worry about her stalker anymore. The man wasn't just a Nazi; he was psychotic."

"We can't forget that he was also being blackmailed," said Harry. "That might have been the reason."

When they reached the Georgian mansion, they found Daphne hunched in the corner of the sofa in the library, looking wholly quenched.

The professor was almost manic in his indignation. "Apparently, the photographs he took of Dafna when she wasn't aware hung all over his apartment," Dr. Adler said. "He had his second bathroom set up as a darkroom. And they've taken the threatening notes Dafna kept to check for a match with the typewriter in Grossman's apartment."

Catherine grimaced and felt sick. "What a twisted man."

Buck, looking every inch the avenger, said, "Of course he was twisted. He worshipped Hitler. Daphne is very lucky he never succeeded in carrying out his threats."

"The police will be back in the morning," said the professor. "They were not at all happy that Dafna failed to report that she had been followed and threatened. They will have compared the typewriter to the notes by then." The professor was up and pacing the room. "Buck has called his doctor to come over and give Daphne a sedative. She will never sleep otherwise."

Through all of this, Daphne did not say a word. Catherine seated herself next to the actress, but Daphne acted as though Catherine weren't even there. The professor began speaking emphatically to Harry in German so Catherine could not understand. Harry spoke back to him in his language.

Buck said to Catherine, "He's afraid the police will be back to arrest Daphne."

When the doctor arrived, Catherine said to Daphne, "Why don't we go upstairs and get you settled in bed before you have your injection. Then you will be all ready to go to sleep. Sleep will be the best thing for you right now."

The actress rose, and Catherine helped her to her bedroom at the head of the stairs.

Daphne finally spoke, "Thank you, Catherine. You can go now. I can undress myself. Tell the doctor I'll be ready for him in ten minutes."

After the doctor went up, the professor seemed calmer. Harry told him they would be back in the morning.

* * *

By the time they got back to the inn, it was after 5:00. Catherine had been mostly silent on the way home. Now she paced the lounge's carpet in a circle. "Think about it, Harry. They're far more likely to arrest Buck than Daphne. If he found out what Grossman had been doing, I imagine his first instinct would have been to break the man's neck."

"Yes. Buck isn't the type to blackmail. He would have gone straight for his throat." Harry said. "Always supposing he knew what Grossman was up to."

Harry cursed.

Catherine said, "I can't help thinking that blackmail is important, but I can't see how it fits in anywhere."

Harry cursed again.

* * *

The following morning, Catherine and Harry arrived at Buck's home at nine o'clock, hoping they weren't too early but wanting to be there early enough to beat the police if they were indeed on their way.

Ames showed them into the library where the professor was trying to read the account of the murder in the morning paper. A full ashtray sat on the desk, and a heavy fug of cigarette smoke weighted the air. Dr. Adler's shirt was deeply creased, and Catherine realized that he hadn't been to bed.

"Have you heard from the police?" she asked.

"Not yet," he said. "But it's only a matter of time. I imagine that as soon as they get a list of those who attended the ANL meeting at the library Saturday night, they will be here directly. I understand that the library is right next door to where they found Grossman's body. We got separated, so I can't even be an alibi for her."

Catherine's heart went out to him. Desperately thinking to find something to mitigate his gloom, she said, "Plenty of other people at that meeting would have wished Grossman dead," she said. "We have heard he was being blackmailed."

"Hmph," was all he answered.

At that moment, Buck joined them. "Daphne is having a bit of a lie-in. That sedative is still doing its work."

After a minute or two of small talk, Catherine asked, "Was Helmut Grossman ever on the set during the time he was trying to convince Michael Fields to direct his movie?"

"As a matter of fact," said Buck, "He came and went over a week's time. Now I figure that's when he developed his fixation on Daphne. We figured out the notes started then."

"What was he like?" Catherine asked. "I only met him once."

Buck lit a cigarette and sat down. The grooves in his face between his mouth and nose seemed to have grown deeper. "He knew better than to talk on the set. Very proper. He didn't call any of us by our given names. It was always Mr. or Miss."

"I suppose he was very disappointed by Mr. Mayer's decision?" she asked.

"He was angry, but he seemed to keep a lid on it. Michael

informed him one day after the shooting was done. Grossman walked straight out and never came back." He flicked cigarette ash into the overflowing ashtray.

"Interesting," Catherine said, discreetly rubbing her fore-head where a headache was developing. She hadn't slept much. "Certainly, Mayer's decision would have only increased the animus he felt toward Jews."

"Did he have much conversation with Daphne?" she asked.

"He followed her with his eyes. He was always watching her," Buck took a long drag on his cigarette. "I admit it bothered me. I'm surprised I never figured out that he was behind those threats. He probably even followed Daphne and Dr. Adler to the meeting Saturday night."

There was a loud knock at the door. They heard Ames answer it. After a few moments, the butler came into the study. "The police are here, Mr. Danforth. They want to see Miss Daphne."

Catherine didn't hesitate. "I'll bring her down," she said. She had no idea which room the actress slept in, but she wasn't going to let Dr. Adler or Buck strategize with her. The police would be able to infer that in an instant.

"And who might you be?" A policeman—of stumpy build with roaring red hair--intercepted her as she made for the stairs.

"I'm Miss Tregowyn," she said. "A friend of the family. The doctor gave Miss Binoche a sedative last night. I will wake her and see that she comes down immediately."

* * *

Daphne was hard to awaken. Beside her bed in the gloom, Catherine was able to discern a bottle of sleeping pills. She must have drugged herself on top of the sedative.

Obviously, an intervention was necessary. Catherine walked to the window and jerked open the drapes. Sunlight flooded Daphne's room.

When the actress finally struggled to consciousness, Catherine whispered, "Sorry to wake you. It's the police. I'm afraid you must rouse yourself. They want to talk to you."

The actress stared at Catherine, and she could sense her processing the words.

She sat up suddenly. "I'm not going to talk to them. Not without Mr. Westerman, my attorney." She slipped out of bed and walked in the direction of the bathroom. "Would you be a dear and call him for me? His card's there by the bed. I spoke to him for a long time last night."

Catherine picked up the phone and rang the attorney at his office. His secretary asked her to hold for him. When Mr. Westerman was on the line, Catherine identified herself. "You met me at the jail when you were there to see Miss Binoche. She has asked me to ring you. She just woke up, and the police are here to see her about the Grossman murder, but she said she won't talk to them without you here."

"Yes. Those were my instructions," the lawyer said. "I'll come over there now. It will take me a while. I'm downtown. Please make certain she doesn't talk to the police before I arrive."

"Thank you, Mr. Westerman, I'll tell her."

Knocking on the bathroom door, she said, "Mr. Westerman is on his way. Will you be all right if I go back downstairs?"

"It will take me a bit to get my face on," the actress said. "I'll meet you downstairs in about twenty minutes."

* * *

The stocky red-haired policeman was accompanied by a small dark partner with narrowly set eyes and a Lenin goatee. The redhead looked up at her entrance. "Miss Binoche?"

"She will be down shortly, but she said she wouldn't speak to you until her lawyer arrived," said Catherine. "He's on his way from downtown."

The bearded policeman raised his brows but said nothing.

Buck said to Catherine, "The threatening notes were a match with Grossman's typewriter."

She nodded. It would have been vastly surprising if they were not.

"I would appreciate it if you could tell us what your connection is to all of this," said the redhead. "Why are you here?"

The professor spoke up. "It is at my insistence," he said. "They are intimate friends of mine from Europe."

Neither Harry nor Catherine thought it wise to add to the professor's explanation. There were things she was dying to know, but she knew she and Harry were only there on the police's sufferance and thought it wise not to make waves.

"Did you know the murdered man?" asked Officer "Goatee."

"I met him once," said Catherine. "He caused quite a stir in the community with his politics, I understand."

"I'm not surprised," said the other policeman. "But it's pretty extreme to go about murdering people because of their politics. In this country, at least. We're searching for another motive."

Catherine thought of Del and said, "I see. So, you're not interested in the members of the Anti-Nazi League who met at the library Saturday night?"

"Not unless they have another association with the victim," Officer Goatee said.

The other policeman looked at his watch. "We need to get going here. Is there a room we can use for our interviews, Mr. Danforth?"

"I can show you through to the study when you are ready."

"Let's start with you then," Officer Redhead said.

Buck showed them to his study, and the professor lit a cigarette with shaking hands. Catherine couldn't begin to imagine what the man was going through. A week here in this foreign country, and already he was probably a suspect in a murder investigation. And all that was on top of his real worry—Daphne.

Mr. Westerman arrived while the police were in with Buck, and

Daphne came down a few minutes later. She took her lawyer into the morning room.

Catherine was restless. There was a feel to the American policemen that was different from what she was used to. She couldn't put her finger on the reason why, but they frightened her. Perhaps because they seemed a bit ruthless?

I'm thinking too much of the Wild West. Those blasted cowboy movies.

Buck emerged, looking shaken. "Where is Daphne?" he asked.

"She's in the morning room with Mr. Westerman," Harry said.

"Well, she's wanted, and I think their patience with her is at an end," Buck said and headed off to the morning room. Moments later, Catherine heard them in the hall as they walked by the open library door.

". . . don't try to be anything but straightforward . . ." Buck was saying.

Westerman cut in, "I will advise Miss Binoche."

The professor had half risen from his chair, but as Buck immediately entered, he sat down.

"What was it like?" the older man asked.

"They're sharp," Buck said. Taking out his handkerchief, he wiped his brow and upper lip. "As soon as they started their questions, I felt automatically guilty. I can't imagine what kind of impression I made."

"Are these the same policemen who are dealing with the Fields' murder?" asked Catherine.

"Yes. Because Daphne is involved—even if only as a victim—they must have decided the two might be linked," said Buck. "I think it's an absurd conclusion myself."

Buck's motive was clear—protecting Daphne—but Catherine was dying to know his alibi.

As though reading her mind, he said, "The thing is, I have no alibi for Saturday night. I didn't feel like going to the club without Daph. I just stayed home and looked over a script my agent sent me. I got rather involved in it and didn't even notice the time."

"Surely the servants can speak for you," said Harry.

"I gave them the night off," he said.

"Hmm," said Catherine. "Difficult."

The professor lit another cigarette from the butt of the first. His eyes were red and his jaw unshaven. He looked a perfect wreck. She wanted to tell him to go upstairs, wash, shave, and change clothes but felt that it was not her place. Daphne could have told him, but Daphne had been completely wrapped up in her own problems.

They sat in silence. Harry filled his pipe and smoked. Soon the air was so full of smoke Catherine thought she might scream.

"I'm going out for a breath of air," she said, rising.

She went across the hall to the drawing room and through the terrace doors into the garden. When she left the shade of the terrace, the heat was stifling, and there wasn't a breath of wind. She needed to walk, however. Pacing the lawn, she wondered what the police were asking Daphne that was taking so long.

Finally, Harry opened the terrace door and said, "She's come out, darling. The professor's with the police now."

* * *

Daphne was sitting next to Buck on the sofa. His hand was over hers as it lay between them.

Her lawyer sat in a corner watching her as she was saying, ". . . they asked me if I was at the ANL meeting Saturday night. Since I was seen by about a hundred and fifty people, I had to say yes. I didn't even know that Grossman was my stalker. Why would I kill him?"

His voice strained, Harry asked, "Can you prove that?"

"How can you prove a negative?" she asked.

Mr. Westerman said, "The police can't prove it one way or another either."

So engaged were they in their speculations, they almost didn't notice when her father came out of the study, followed by the police. The professor was looking mulish.

"We are taking Dr. Adler down to the station with us for further questioning," said Officer Goatee.

Catherine's heart fell in dismay. *No. Not the professor!*

Daphne sprang up from the sofa. "Papa? No! Of course, he didn't do it! Mr. Westerman! Go with him!"

"Miss Binoche, I cannot represent both of you. It is a conflict of interest."

"Dafna," said her father, "I do not need an attorney. All will be well, *meinen Schatz.*"

"I will come with you, then!" the actress said, tears falling down her face.

"No," said the policeman. "We will talk to him alone."

Chapter Seventeen

Catherine had never seen Daphne so agitated. The tears she cried now weren't beautiful. Her eyes were red, and her nose was running. She turned to Catherine.

"You must *do* something!" she said. "You know Papa wouldn't kill that man!"

"Does your father even know how to shoot?" Catherine asked. "I can't picture that."

Daphne bit her lip. "If they contact Vienna, they will find that he is a member of the *Schutzbund!*" In her agitation she stood, looking around her as though she suspected the police of hiding behind the bookshelves.

"What's the *Schutzbund*, darling?" asked Buck.

"It's the Austrian Socialist Party's private army. He's been a member since the War. But Papa wouldn't kill that man. Why would he? He didn't know he was my stalker. None of us did!"

"You have a valid point," said Harry rising from his casual seat on the arm of Catherine's overstuffed chair. "But would he confess to protect you, Daphne?"

Dejected, the actress sat again, and, putting her hands over her face, she continued weeping. "Yes. He would. He would. What can we do?"

Catherine looked at the dispirited woman. She wondered if

she completely understood her father's danger. Grossman was a Nazi who had threatened his daughter with murder because she was Jewish. He was a Jewish socialist who belonged to an army of socialists.

Mr. Westerman spoke up, "Your father needs an attorney. I'll contact Mayer's people and get in touch with you this afternoon."

The actress turned to her lawyer. "Oh! Could you, Mr. Westerman? That would be such a help."

The lawyer acknowledged her gratitude and said, "I'll be going then."

Harry said to Daphne, "Your father loves you and probably thinks what he is doing is the only way he can protect you. You were already framed for Fields' murder. You are still under arrest for that. He can't do anything to help you there, so he is helping the only way he thinks he can."

"Do you think it's the same person who murdered Michael?" Daphne asked. "Do you think by killing Grossman where he did, the murderer is trying to frame me again?"

"That's a good question," said Catherine. "I can't imagine it being the same person, though. The only thing that the two murders have in common is you. One man ostensibly hated you; one man loved you."

The actress said, "The only people I can think of that hate me that much are Michael's family. And they wouldn't have any motive for killing Herr Grossman."

Catherine shuffled and sorted the facts in her head. Were the cases related?

"Daphne, did you leave the ANL meeting at any time? Even for a little while?"

The woman licked her lips and closed her eyes as she thought about the question. "After Del finished speaking, I did go to the powder room. I ran into a friend there, and we spoke for a few minutes."

"How long were you away? Could your friend give you an alibi?"

Daphne took a deep breath and released it in a heavy sigh. "Probably fifteen or twenty minutes. I don't even know where she lives. I only know her from the ANL."

Harry stood up and paced. He said, "You should ask Mr. Westerman to put someone on that."

Daphne said, "I only know her as April. I don't even know her last name."

"Doesn't the ANL have records?" asked Harry.

"No. Nothing is written. They don't trust the police. We pay dues on the honor system. Meetings are announced openly."

"I'd still see what he can do."

Harry took his pipe out of his jacket pocket and beat the bowl against his palm. "So, unless he turns up April, you have a twenty-minute gap in your alibi. What about your father? Have you any idea where he was?"

"He was joining up. He was off in a room with some other people. I don't even know who they were. He might. But if he's just posing as the killer, he won't say who they are."

Catherine had been thinking. "What was Grossman doing at the library at that hour anyway?"

Daphne said, "He certainly wasn't hobnobbing with the Anti-Nazi League. After I learned about the photographs, I assumed he was there because he had been stalking me." She shuddered and pinched her lips together.

Catherine thought this through. "But if that were true," she said, "The killer wouldn't have known Grossman would be there. Don't you think it's more likely that Grossman had an appointment with someone? Someone who was at the meeting?"

Hyacinth thought it was his blackmailer, but how did that make sense?

"We've got to find another motive for his murder besides protecting Daphne. Who else would want to kill Grossman?" asked Harry as he filled his pipe. "Was the murder set up where it was to implicate a member of the ANL?"

Catherine looked at her watch. Dot's train was due. They

needed to get to the station. The timing was terrible. She felt like they were on the right track, and she hated to leave. She apologized to Daphne, "My friend's train from Chicago is due. I have to go pick her up at the station. We'll be in touch."

* * *

Dot was in fine form and a breath of fresh air. She ran across the platform to embrace Catherine. "Wonderful to see you, but are you sure this is really Los Angeles? It looks like nothing on earth! We've been coming across the most incredible desert and mountains for days and days. Not to mention endless cornfields."

Catherine laughed. It was so good to see her friend. Dot was dressed in an olive green traveling costume with a matching cloche hat. Her red hair was restrained in a low chignon.

"How did your business go?" Catherine asked.

"It went surprisingly well. Lots of interest in my products. Any success in your murder case?"

"I'll tell you all about it on the way to the inn. Here comes your porter, I think."

Harry greeted Dot and led the porter through the station. The Chevrolet waited by the curb.

"I hope you don't mind," Catherine said. "Max is very anxious to see you, so we're all going out to dinner tonight."

Dot stopped in her tracks. "Max? You're talking about Maxwell Jones? I thought he was engaged!"

"Trouble there, I think. He really wants to see you."

Her friend frowned. "Well, I don't know why. There's no future in it."

"Let's just have a good time, all right?"

"Fine with me," said Dot. "Wow. I love these palm trees."

As they drove from downtown L.A. to Westwood, Catherine explained Mission-style architecture and the surprisingly small UCLA campus.

"I have a class tomorrow morning," she said. "It seems like

ages since last Thursday. There was another murder on Saturday night. We don't know if it's related to the first one, but some of the same people are involved."

"Of course," said Dot. "I should have known. What did you expect?"

"Don't worry. You'll get to meet some famous people. Unfortunately, our professor friend is being held at the police station for the latest murder. I'm fairly certain he's innocent. Here we are. This is the inn."

"Well, just let me take a real shower, and you can tell me the details over lunch. I don't suppose there's a pub?"

"Nothing like that here. There's a fabulous delicatessen, however."

"Will it make up for the one we missed in New York?" asked Dot as she walked into the inn.

"I think so. And that reminds me, I must catch you up on Lady N."

"She's here?" asked Dot.

Catherine nodded, and her friend walked to the check-in desk.

* * *

While Dot showered, Catherine and Harry discussed their conversation at Buck's and relaxed in her sitting room. "You know, Buck is every bit as good a suspect for the murder as the professor," she said. "And whatever the police say, with the ANL in the vicinity, I still think there's a possibility the murder may have a political angle."

Harry surprised her by pulling her into his arms and kissing her ear.

"Darling," she protested. "I'm trying to concentrate."

"I'm concentrating, as well. You have intriguing ears. Have I ever told you that?" He outlined her ear with his finger. Her whole body tingled.

"What if it was Del?" she blurted out.

Giving the ear a final kiss, he said, "That conclusion has an air of desperation to it."

"Well, he was there. He hated Grossman, and I'm certain he despises Daphne."

"You haven't convinced me. It's early days yet," Harry said with an aggrieved sigh. "But I sure hate to think of poor Dr. Adler in that stinking jail if they go ahead and arrest him."

Dot entered the lounge, her bouncy self, her auburn hair in its customary shoulder-length curls. She wore an attractive new ivory dress.

"Darling, you look stunning," said Catherine. "I'm so glad you're here."

To her surprise, just as they were ready to leave for the delicatessen, Daphne walked into the lounge. She went straight to Catherine, who hardly recognized her behind oversized sunglasses and a floppy sunhat.

"I'm sorry," the actress said. "I didn't know where else to turn. *Je suis tres éperdue,*"

When she removed the sunglasses, Catherine saw that she was crying. Her momentary annoyance switched to alarm. She threw a look at Harry, then looked at Dot.

He said, "We'll wait for you at the delicatessen."

Catherine said, "Thank you." Turning to Daphne, she said. "Why don't we go back to my sitting room?"

When they reached her room, she asked the actress, "May I make you some tea? There's a gas ring here."

"*Non, merci.*"

"I doubt that my French is equal to yours," Catherine said. "Do you mind speaking English? What has upset you?"

"It is Buck. I'm terribly afraid he murdered that horrible man. I found out he hired a detective! He knew my stalker was Herr Grossman. He found out on Thursday!"

"Buck told you this?"

"No. I found the report in his desk in the study. I was looking for a pen. I don't know what to do." She bit her bottom lip hard.

"Catherine, I love my father. But I don't want to tell the police about Buck." The actress covered her face with her hands. "He can't be a murderer, can he?" she asked, her voice plaintive as a child's. "He's cruel, but I don't think he's a murderer."

"I'm afraid it makes a great deal of sense," Catherine said. Standing, she nipped into the bathroom and brought out a box of tissues to take the place of Daphne's sodden handkerchief. The actress pulled out a handful and blew her nose.

As Daphne continued to cry, her shoulders curled over her chest, Catherine thought back to her aborted dinner with Buck.

"Daphne, you must tell me the truth. Were you really in love with Mr. Fields? Was that confession you made to Harry and me the truth? Buck told me it was all acting."

Sitting up suddenly, her face blank with puzzlement, she said, "He did? Buck said that?"

Catherine nodded.

"It wasn't acting. I'm afraid it was very cruel to Buck, but he already knew."

Stomach knotting, Catherine leaned forward and said gently, "If you're telling me the truth, then Buck lied to me. This is very serious. I'm afraid he has a motive for both murders. You must see that."

Daphne rubbed the skin behind her neck. There was a little tic by her mouth as muscles jumped under her skin. Catherine wished she were more skilled at reading people. Daphne was far more emotional than anyone she had ever dealt with, but she didn't know whether the emotion was genuine. She wished Harry were here.

"I see it," Daphne said, her voice small and tight. "But I don't know whether to believe it."

Catherine moved to the chair next to Daphne's and put her hand on the woman's knee. "Are you willing to have your father arrested when you have this knowledge about Buck's potential guilt?"

"No. I don't know. I just thought . . ." Daphne paused,

pinching the bridge of her nose. "I just thought maybe you could prove Buck's innocence."

Catherine took a deep breath. "But what if he's guilty? Where does Buck think you are right now?"

"I don't know. He said he had to go out for a while. That's when I found the report. I came in a taxi."

"Look, Daphne," Catherine said finally. "For your father's sake and for your own, I think the sooner you tell the police about the detective's report, the better it will be. I'll go with you if you like."

Daphne linked her fingers together tightly and brought her knuckles up to her lips. "That would be a huge betrayal. And he's done so much for me."

"Buck isn't going to be happy. It's true he's devoted to you, but because of the things you know, you're a danger to him. And you must think of your poor father." Catherine understood her anguish. But how could she make the woman see the truth? "Buck's almost pathologically possessive, Daphne. Such people can be dangerous."

Daphne's brow was furled, her eyes pleading, "But if he's so crazy over me, why would he set me up for Michael's murder? If he committed that, he went out of the way to use my pistol."

Catherine had completely forgotten about that detail. She sighed with frustration. "You're right. It doesn't make sense. But I doubt that the police will see it that way."

"I think that changes everything," said Daphne. "I'm not ready to go to the police. Some of the facts fit, but that one doesn't. Can we agree that I will move out of the house, but we won't go to the police yet?"

Catherine threw her hands up in the air. "But what about your father?" she asked. "You know as well as I do that he's just trying to protect you! He didn't kill Grossman."

"You're right," Daphne said, bringing her fists to her temples. "Oh! It's all so confusing!"

Catherine tried to be calm, though Daphne's angst was contagious. "Are you going to sacrifice your father for Buck?"

CHAPTER EIGHTEEN

In the end, Daphne realized she could not keep the detective's report to herself. She needed to give the police the facts. She could not let her father manufacture them. Though her heart was heavy and protesting, she agreed to go with Catherine to the police.

They ordered a taxi.

* * *

The police station was a gray cement block structure—strictly utilitarian. When they entered, a young officer behind a desk greeted them.

"We have some information on the Grossman murder," Catherine said. "It's rather important."

"I will call through to Detective Davies," the officer said. "Your names?"

Catherine told him, and moments later, the red-headed policeman entered the waiting room.

"Have you come about your father?" he asked Daphne. "His lawyer is with him."

"I have some important information for you," the actress said. "Is there somewhere private?"

The detective took them down the gray hall with its portraits of what looked to be a succession of Police Commissioners. They entered a stifling, windowless, pistachio green room. The ceiling fan was not on. Catherine was already uncomfortable.

Detective Davies left them there for a moment and returned with a colorless woman who held a stenographer's pad. She seated herself in the corner. The policeman took a chair across from where Daphne and Catherine sat, side by side.

"All right. What do you have to tell me?" he asked, his voice weary as he leaned back in his chair.

Daphne seemed to have drawn into herself. She remained speechless. Catherine wet her lips and began to speak. "About an hour ago, Miss Binoche came to the inn where I am staying. She had made an unpleasant discovery and was quite upset."

The detective leaned forward, his face impassive and hard. "Did you find the gun, Miss Binoche?" he asked.

His words shocked Daphne into speech. "Oh, no. Nothing like that. I was in Mr. Danforth's desk, looking for a pen when I found a report from a private detective."

"Oh, yeah? Go on."

"Apparently, Mr. Danforth had hired him to find out who was stalking me. He found out it was Mr. Grossman."

A light went on in the detective's eyes. "And do you happen to remember the name of this detective?"

"Joseph Banks," Daphne murmured.

"Joe. Okay. Good." The detective looked almost jovial.

"The significance of this is that Mr. Danforth is deeply in love with Miss Binoche," said Catherine.

"Yes," said the policeman. "I had gathered that. Well. Well." The detective studied Daphne for a moment. "I guess I wouldn't have expected you to run right into the police station with this information."

"It's my father," Daphne choked out. "I wouldn't have said anything, but you know that my father didn't know that Herr Grossman was my stalker. He had no motive to kill him."

"But your boyfriend does."

Daphne broke down in sobs. Catherine handed her a clean handkerchief.

"You say you found this report in the desk drawer. Could you be more specific? We're going to need to go in with a search warrant."

Daphne specified which drawer and then asked, "Could I please go now? And can my father go?"

"We had decided that he knew far too little of the crime to be our perp," the detective said. "The paperwork should be done now. I'll have him released to you out in the front room if you ladies can wait a few more minutes."

Daphne uttered a low moan as she realized she needn't have told the police anything.

To Catherine's surprise, the detective said, "It wasn't all for nothing. This gives your boyfriend a chance to clear himself. We suspected him, you know."

This was cold comfort.

* * *

"I can't possibly go back to Buck's after what I've done," said Daphne as they left the police station with her father.

He said something in German to his daughter. She replied in the same language. Then, to Catherine, she said, "I'm going to the inn to stay instead of my house. Could we take my father there so he can shower and nap? Then, if you would be so good, we could go to my house, and I could pack up some things, so I won't have to go back to Buck's."

"That sounds like a good plan, agreed Catherine. "Harry and I will need to consult with you on the investigation into the Fields murder."

"It would definitely make me feel better. I do have to face Buck on the set, however."

Their cab pulled up to the curb at the inn.

* * *

Catherine could easily see why Daphne preferred her authentic Mission-style residence in San Gabriel to the neo-Georgian house where Buck lived. The neighborhood, however, left much to be desired. There were run-down commercial businesses all up and down the street.

They were greeted by a tiny Hispanic woman dressed in gray with a white apron.

"Señorita! At last, you have come home!"

"Not to stay, Emma. Only to pick up a few things. Then I go with my friend, Señorita Tregowyn. I will be at the Westwood Inn if you need anything."

The inside of the home with its tile floors and vaulted ceilings was well restored. It looked as though Daphne was still in the midst of furnishing it with wood and canvas furniture. Colorful Indian rugs dressed the white walls.

Daphne, with her maid's help, collected armfuls of clothing and quickly packed them into a large steamer trunk. She added toiletries, perfume, and make-up to the tray that fit inside. In twenty minutes, they went out to the waiting cab and asked the driver to bring the trunk. Soon they were on their way to Westwood.

"I think the sooner we resume our investigation of the Fields murder, the better you will feel, Daphne. We can no longer control where the Grossman investigation goes, but we have unexplored avenues in your director's murder. Let's concentrate on that, shall we?"

"That's a good idea, but I am drained right now. It has been an awful day. I am going to take a hot bath and go to bed early."

"I think that's a good idea," said Catherine. "It has been an emotional time for you, and no wonder." She let a few quiet seconds go by before she asked, "Is there any way you can call into the Starlight Club and give instructions to let our party in tonight? I think that is the best place to continue our investigations. That is probably where your gun went missing."

"Yes," said Daphne as the cab pulled up in front of the inn. "I will do it, but I am so weary of all of this!"

"It is wearisome, I agree."

* * *

Harry was in the lounge with Dot and very glad to see her. Once Daphne had her room, Catherine joined her friends in the lounge. She brought them up to date on the events of her afternoon.

"I think going to the police to inform them of Buck's knowing Grossman was her stalker was the most difficult thing she ever had to do. She did it for her father; otherwise, I don't think she would have gone." She turned to her friend. "Harry has told you about the two murders, I assume?"

Dot said, "Harry has spent the entire afternoon trying to do that. I only hope I have everything straight."

"Daphne is calling ahead to get us into the club tonight, but she is far too dispirited to join us," Catherine told them. To Dot, she said, "I hope you're in the mood for a nightclub with great jazz and lots of movie stars."

"Ooo. Of course!" said Dot. "So, will we go there after dinner with Max?"

"That's what I'd like to do," said Catherine.

"Sounds like a great time."

* * *

Max showed up at the inn at seven o'clock. Catherine didn't know exactly what to expect of him in the situation.

The "cowboy" carried it off with tremendous aplomb, to her surprise. He held Dot by the shoulders and inspected her from head to toe with a huge grin on his face. "Good thing we're going out to dinner, 'cause you look good enough to eat," he said. "I've missed you like the Dickens."

"And what about your fiancée?" Dot asked.

"We're taking a little break," he said. "I'm footloose at the moment."

Dot just looked at him, then she warmed them all with her smile, and they went to pile themselves into the Chevrolet.

Because it was such a "California experience," they had dinner at the Brown Derby. Dot marveled at the restaurant in the shape of a hat. "Are you sure the food is edible?" she asked.

"It's great," Max assured her. He showed her the caricatures of the actors. "Their steak is the best in town," he told Dot.

They all ordered the steak.

Conversation was general to begin with, but eventually, they began discussing the latest murder. There amidst the white linen tablecloths and wood-paneled walls, they broached theories and reluctantly dismissed them. Max said he had always distrusted Buckingham Danforth because he was too good-looking to be true. Dot, not dissuaded by the lack of evidence, thought Ruth Fields was the villain for the first murder and had no ideas about the second. Catherine admitted she was completely at sea, but something was trying to tell her that Delano Fields was involved. Harry put his money on Daphne, to everyone's surprise.

"What?" he said when Catherine protested. "She's absolutely the only one who fits in every particular. I can't help it if she's the most obvious. The woman's a narcissist."

"They all are," said Catherine. "That's part of the problem. Still, she did save her father this afternoon. At the expense of Buck. I feel a bit low making a game of all of this."

"If we didn't, we'd all be mad by now," Harry said, then changed the topic. "Have you got your dancing shoes on, Max? We're going to the Starlight Club after dinner to see if we can further our investigation. That's one of the places the murderer could have got hold of Daphne's weapon."

Max's eyes lit, and he looked at Dot. "I meant to ask you if we could go dancing. That's one of my favorite memories of Oxford—the time we spent dancing."

* * *

Hyacinth and Joe Calloway were sitting in their habitual booth. To Catherine's surprise, Ruth Fields was with Calloway. Catherine suspected they were holding hands under the table. Harry introduced them to Dot and Max, who promptly moved out on the floor and began dancing.

Hyacinth had obviously recovered from the shock of Grossman's death. Was she putting up a brave front, or had she merely been stringing the Nazi along so she could get a role in his film? Catherine thought it was probably the latter.

Buck arrived. *How long did it take to get a search warrant?* Either he had not heard from the police, or he was employing brilliant acting skills, for he was accompanied by Lady Naomi and seemed in the best of spirits.

Harry looked at Catherine. She rolled her eyes at him, definitely not in the mood for Lady N.

Buck hailed everyone and said, "We are celebrating! Lady Naomi just had a brilliant screen test today with John Hale. You are looking at Hollywood's next big star!"

Joe Calloway said under his breath, "Well, la di da!"

Hyacinth pouted, "Wonderful! More competition."

The jazz number ended, and Max and Dot returned to the table. Harry performed introductions.

Addressing the group at large, Lady Naomi asked, "Has anyone seen Daphne? She has disappeared! I know she would want to hear my news."

Harry and Catherine had agreed to feign ignorance. Buck asked Dot to dance. She acquiesced, and Joe Calloway asked Catherine.

The villain seemed to be in a jolly mood. "I take it you are not a fan of Queen Naomi?"

"I think she'll make a smashing actress," said Catherine ambivalently. "She has all the right instincts."

Calloway laughed. "Narcissism. Right you are." He led her

smoothly for a few moments, then said, "I understand you're quite the Sherlock Holmes. Who d'you think murdered the Nazi?"

"I've no idea," she said, dancing an automatic foxtrot. "Did you ever meet him?"

"Oh, yes. He hung around the set at the studio for a while. As you Brits would say, he was a rum fellow." Calloway's pencil mustache seemed to quiver as though there were an unpleasant odor.

"He'd been stalking Daphne," said Catherine, trying to relax into the dance and failing. She felt stiff, like a hunting dog *en pointe*.

"You don't say! Grossman, eh? That's a bit of a surprise."

"She's very upset. You know they took her father in for questioning this morning?"

"He's a bit of a Red, like Daphne, I'll bet."

"He's not a Communist. He's a socialist. That's a bona fide political party in Austria."

He gave her a sour look. "Jews."

She ignored him and wished the dance was over.

"It's not like Daphne to miss a night at the club," her partner said. "She must be fonder of her father than I realized."

"I believe them to be quite close," said Catherine. "How is your movie coming along with your new director?"

Calloway gave a slight shake of his head. "He's definitely second rate. I'm afraid we're missing Fields' brilliance."

"I wish I'd been able to meet him," said Catherine. "From all accounts, he seems to have been a remarkable man."

"Yes," he said, twirling her and bending her backward over his arm.

The move surprised Catherine. He went on, "That doesn't mean he was a saint, however."

Catherine said, "But then neither was his widow, was she?"

For a moment, his face went still, and then he smiled, and his eyes actually sparkled. For the first time, Catherine saw his charm. "There's a saying about gooses and ganders enjoying the same sauce, isn't there?"

"Who do you think the murderer is?" she asked.

"Probably someone no one has even thought of—Agatha Christie-style."

Catherine thought of the divorce evidence sitting in Fields' office. She wondered suddenly if Fields had had a life insurance policy with Ruth as his beneficiary. But then that probably wasn't a factor. Calloway was "loaded," and didn't Ruth have "old money?"

She decided she would have a little fun with this man who seemed to like needling her. "Well, at least Ruth Fields doesn't need to worry about losing the life insurance," she said.

"Are you implying that that was a motive for murder? Fields wasn't going to divorce her!"

"Oh yes, he was," Catherine said with the naughty grin she could pull up when the occasion warranted it. "There's proof, but that's all I'm allowed to say."

Joe Calloway looked utterly flummoxed.

She laughed.

"You are Sherlock Holmes, aren't you?"

Fortunately, the dance ended. Catherine did not even wait to be escorted back to the table. She marched off, anxious to be reunited with Dot and Harry. It had felt good to turn the tables on Mr. Joseph Calloway for once.

A new guest had joined them. Catherine was almost relieved to see Richard Darcy, rigged out in full evening dress with a red carnation in his buttonhole.

"Well?" she prompted him. "Have you got the newest murder solved yet?"

"Of course," he said. "Grossman was done to death by an elderly lady of independent means who had a squint and dyed her hair blonde."

Catherine grinned. "She was a Communist, of course."

He put a finger to his lips, "Shhh. That's privileged information."

To her surprise, Buck asked her to dance. Wishing she had a convenient excuse, she dithered but ended by accepting his invitation.

"Do you know where Daphne is?" he asked as soon as they were out on the floor.

"Is she missing?" Catherine asked, hoping she looked innocent. Harry frequently told her that her face was an open book. "Perhaps she went to the beach again."

"I've looked all her favorite places. I even checked that crummy hotel where she went last time. Her maid told me she hasn't been home, but I think she was lying. Emma doesn't lie well. If Daphne's run away, I hope she knows she's going to have the police to deal with. Not to mention Louis Mayer, who put up her bail."

"That is strange." Her heart raced. The look in her partner's eyes did not bode well for Daphne. He looked far less like the handsome prince and much more like the Devil.

"There's a killer out there on the loose!" he said, his voice savage. Ames told me the police were at the house with a search warrant. They came while I was out looking for her. I imagine they went through all her things. "How does she expect me to protect her?"

"I wasn't aware that that was your job," said Catherine.

"Daph depends on me to take care of her. She is more scatter-brained than you would believe."

"Well, at least her stalker is no longer around," Catherine tried to sound soothing. "Where were you this afternoon?" he asked, his dark, brooding eyes looking into hers, reminding her of Heathcliff at the end of his tether.

"My dearest friend just came into town. I told you that we were going to pick her up at the station. Then she wanted to go to Sol's."

"Sol's?"

"The delicatessen in Westwood. She was longing to try a Jewish delicatessen. We missed the opportunity in New York." Catherine knew she was babbling.

She became aware that she was afraid. She might be dancing with Grossman's murderer. As she had noted earlier, his feelings for Daphne were obsessive. His hand crushed the hand he held as they danced.

"Maybe Daphne is at the jail visiting her father. I'm sure she didn't feel like dancing tonight," Catherine suggested.

"Visitors are not allowed to stay longer than half an hour," Buck said sharply.

"Well," she said with a sigh, "I'm sorry I can't tell you where she is."

He looked at her balefully and said nothing for the rest of the dance. He was like a puppet, doing the dance steps as though someone else pulled the strings.

She couldn't recall ever being as relieved as she was when the dance ended. Dot was sitting at the table chatting away to Mr. Darcy when Catherine arrived. She crooked her finger at Dot and then mimed powdering her nose. Her friend excused herself and then stood up to follow Catherine to the Ladies' room.

As they stood powdering themselves in front of the large, gilded mirror, Catherine whispered. "If Buck asks you if I was with you this afternoon, I was, all right?"

"All right," Dot assured her. "He's a little intense."

"Borderline psychotic, I'd say," Catherine said.

As they walked back out, "Stormy Weather" was playing, and suddenly a wave of homesickness overtook her. She had sung the song last fall with another jazz band back at Oxford. She missed it. She missed Oxford. These Americans—or faux Americans in the case of Buck—were getting on her nerves. They were a mass of bleeding hearts—Buck with his obsession with Daphne, Joe Calloway with his bitterness. Hyacinth with her ambition. She was tired of the intense emotions eddying around her. She was ready for some comfortable British reticence.

CHAPTER NINETEEN

Tuesday morning, Daphne surprised Catherine and Harry by inviting them to the studio to see the filming.

"I would feel so much better if the two of you were there. I'm really dreading seeing Buck."

Catherine didn't blame her. It was bound to be awkward. Daphne seemed to have lost all her confidence. Unfortunately, she and Harry had class. When she explained this, Catherine said, "Perhaps your father would like to go with you."

This cheered Daphne, and Professor Adler was happy to go. As they left the inn, however, Catherine was alarmed to see that he did not look well. This entire situation was aging him terribly.

When she apologized to Dot for leaving her, she said, "Don't worry. Max is taking me to the seashore!"

* * *

It was good to be back in the classroom again, even this unfamiliar one with its view of undeveloped land. She began the discussion with the question, "What makes *Room With a View* and *Man of Property* essentially English novels? Why could they not take place in America?"

There followed a discussion of both novels' thematic material regarding the class struggle in England, which was not part of life in America except in very rarified circles in the East. The students were very proud of belonging to a "meritocracy," especially in their country's Western states.

A bright student called Ann stated that New England and New York were still bound by the principles of "old money" vs. *nuevo riche* but acknowledged that Los Angeles was much closer to the 'American dream.' A few of the girls brought up Fitzgerald's *The Great Gatsby,* which dealt with the values of New York high society and discussed how those mirrored the old English values.

After discussing the symbolic roles of the two novels' various characters, they then considered how the books differed from those of the Victorian Age. The consensus was that they differed "not all that much."

"As I told you last week, the seminal difference in English literature between the nineteenth and twentieth centuries did not come until after the War, which scorched a path across every aspect of our lives in England. In order to understand what the War meant to our country, I would like you to read *A Testament of Youth* by Vera Brittain. It is a bit lengthy, so that will be the only work we will read this next week. I would like you to write a 500-word essay comparing the life of Vera Brittain and Lucy Honeychurch.

"On Friday night at 8:00, I will be giving a lecture on the British War Poets. I believe you will find it interesting. You are invited to bring whomever you like. My colleague, Dr. Bascombe, will be doing readings from these poets."

After this, class was dismissed. Catherine's heart swelled with pleasure at having connected with her students. The experience was far more satisfying than being in the middle of a murder investigation where emotions ran high, and she never knew what was true and what wasn't.

Meeting Harry in the Dining Hall for lunch, she inquired how his class went.

"It was good. As a result of my lecture on Friday, I had quite a few 'auditors.' I don't know how the administration views that."

"Ah!" Catherine laughed. "Did they giggle?"

"They managed not to commit that breach of decorum!" Harry grinned.

"You have achieved 'star' status," she said. "Your next lecture will be mobbed!"

Harry shook his head. She knew it was a new experience for him to teach impressionable females, and he was possibly a bit embarrassed. He asked, "Any ideas what we should do in our other profession today?"

"Academia is such a nice escape. But Dr. Adler is counting on us," she said, trying to eat her spaghetti in a polite manner. "I feel that I'm getting a bit muddled. I think it's time for us to stop and assess what we know and how it all fits together. Let's go back to the inn."

Upon arrival at their abode, they were greeted by an agitated Daphne.

"The police have Buck at the station for questioning. Filming was canceled. John Hale is absolutely livid, and the cast is fraught."

Daphne's normally smooth hair was frizzy, and she hadn't removed her "stage" makeup making all her features seemed overly large.

"Well," said Catherine. "I guess it was to be expected."

"Is that all you can say?" Daphne screeched. "It's my fault! When he finds out . . ."

"How will he find out? The police won't tell him why they decided to search the house. He was out looking for you when they came. I'm sure he has no idea . . ."

"*Buck knows things. He figures them out.*"

Catherine looked at the woman closely. "You're afraid of him, aren't you? That is what all this is about."

In silence, Daphne pulled off the cotton jacket she wore despite the heat. There, blossoming on her arm, was a grotesque purple bruise the size of a pancake.

Shock rendered Catherine speechless. She sat down with a

thud on the lounge's sofa. Her mouth went dry. Covering her arm again, Daphne sat down next to her.

Finally, Catherine said, "He hits you."

"Yes. And I'm terrified that you're right. I'm afraid that he killed Michael. And Grossman."

"Hopefully, they'll lock him up," said Catherine flatly.

"The picture won't continue now. I'm going back to France. Papa is going with me."

"I don't blame you. But you're still out on bail. Unless the state dismisses charges, you will not be allowed to leave the country. If you try, they'll lock *you* up. You need to talk with your lawyer. Call Mr. Westerman now. You need to be someplace safe."

"So do you, if Buck gets out on bail."

Catherine's neck and palms were moist, and she could feel sweat dripping down between her shoulder blades. Harry entered the lounge.

He must have detected her distress, for he said, "What is it?"

Closing her eyes, Catherine took a deep breath to calm herself. She was getting carried away by Daphne's fears.

"What is it, darling?" she asked him.

He said to Daphne. "I'm afraid your father isn't well." He turned to Catherine, and she read worry on his brow. "He needs a doctor. Possibly an ambulance."

"Papa?" said Daphne. "I must go to him now!"

Without further ado, she leaped to her feet and went running back to his room.

Catherine asked, "What is it?"

"His heart, I'm afraid."

Getting up, Catherine walked to the inn's front desk. A portly man stood there. "How may I help you?"

"We need an ambulance for Dr. Adler immediately," she said. "Inform them it's a possible cardiac arrest."

* * *

Catherine was so worried about Daphne that she rode in the back of the ambulance with her and the professor. The technicians worked around them to hook up the cumbersome electrocardiogram. Dr. Adler was now breathing through an oxygen mask and had an IV in his arm.

When they pulled up to the county hospital, more technicians poured out the doors and rolled the gurney into the emergency room. Catherine and Daphne followed. Harry was driving on his own in the Chevrolet.

Because Catherine wasn't family, she was prohibited from going back into the trauma room. She stayed behind on a hard chair in the waiting room. Harry joined her minutes later.

"I wouldn't have had this happen for the world," he said. "We should have been watching for something like this."

"We couldn't know he had heart problems, but I was worried about him this morning. He didn't look well when he left for the studio."

"At least Daphne's safe here in the hospital," said Harry. "I wonder whether Buck is under arrest."

"Mr. Westerman could find out," said Catherine. "I feel like we should ring him."

"I'll go find a public telephone," said Harry.

* * *

Daphne didn't reappear until 6:00 pm. There was no need to worry about the press here, fortunately. She wasn't looking her best.

"They've stabilized him. It looks like he's going to make it. I just came down to tell you to go back to the inn. I'm staying the night here," Daphne told them, winding her hands together. "There's an extra bed in the ward where he is. If he makes it through the night, his chances are good. I feel terrible that I've done this to him. I should have listened to him. He wanted me to stay in France."

"We'll go if you promise to ring us if there's a change," Catherine said. She decided Daphne did not need to know the latest from Mr. Westerman. Buck had not been arrested. He had the best criminal lawyer in the business.

* * *

"So where does this leave us?" asked Harry as they drove back to the inn.

"To me, it looks more and more like Buck is guilty," Catherine said.

Harry agreed, and so it was with consternation that they found Buck waiting for them at the inn.

His jaw was rigid with anger as he grabbed Catherine by the arm. "What have you done with Daphne?" he demanded.

Wrenching her arm away, she confronted him. "Professor Adler has had a severe heart attack. He is in critical condition. Daphne is with him and is going to spend the night at the hospital. You will not be welcome there. I suggest you take your bad temper and leave."

Harry clapped a hand on Buck's shoulder. "Now," he said.

"Is he dying?" the actor asked.

"It is too soon to tell," said Harry. "Now go."

Buck pulled his jacket straight, composed his features, and left.

"Phew!" said Catherine.

They sat in the lounge and ordered coffee. There was a message for them from Dot that she and Max had gone dancing.

The words brought a smile to Catherine's face, and she relaxed a bit. "Things are obviously going well in that quarter. I'm glad. We've hardly had a word with Dot."

"Max isn't wasting any time," Harry said.

They sat for a few moments in silence. Catherine's head was full of ideas.

"Where do we go from here?" she said.

"We should probably try to help build the case against Buck."

"Daphne feels he is guilty of both murders. I feel like we're missing something. Something must have brought him to a boil where Fields was concerned. You know what keeps sticking in my mind?"

"I haven't the foggiest, darling. Your mind is an object of wonder to me."

"Seriously, Harry. I keep thinking of all that money that was being paid to 'D.' Do you suppose that D might have meant Danforth and not Del?"

"Do you think we should approach Del and ask him? I can't see him thinking he owes us an answer!"

"No. But Alvira would probably know. I think I will give her a ring right now. It's early still. She's probably working on her assignment for Thursday. It was a hefty one."

"You might as well give it a try," Harry said.

On a hunch, Catherine looked up Ruth's telephone number, as a well-known director probably wouldn't have his name listed in the telephone directory. To her satisfaction, she found it and put the call through from the telephone in the lounge.

The butler asked her, "And who should I say is calling?"

"Miss Tregowyn. I'm her teacher at UCLA."

When Alvira came on the line, Catherine said, "Miss Fields, I would like to ask you a question, if I may. It may seem intrusive, but I am trying to build a case against the person we believe murdered your father."

"Yes. All right," the girl said.

"In your father's bankbook, there are records of large checks written to 'D.' At first glance, I thought that to be your brother, but he told us he was cut off financially."

"You think my brother killed my father?" she said, her words almost sizzling across the line.

"No. He is not our suspect. But we must eliminate him."

"You must not think I am very bright if you think I'll believe that."

Catherine rolled her eyes in Harry's direction.

"Listen, Miss Fields. I do think you're bright. The man we are building the case against also has the initial 'D.'"

"Buck Danforth, you mean?" Now the girl sounded eager.

"You must not share that information with anyone. Not even Lionel."

"Very well. Del used to get a monthly check for $50. That was on top of his tuition, which my father paid at the beginning of every term. But my father cut off his allowance several months ago. He still paid his tuition, but that was all. He paid me a lump sum at the start of every year."

Catherine's heart raced. "Thank you so much, Miss Fields. "Now I have another question for you. Can you think of anything that your father may have been being blackmailed for? Was there any scandal in the family he might have been trying to cover up? I realize this is delicate, but blackmail makes sense under the circumstances; I think you will agree."

"Well, I don't see how that information could apply to his murder," the girl said. "Why would the blackmailer kill Daddy? Shouldn't it be the other way around?"

"I haven't quite figured that out yet, but I think you'll agree that there was something suspicious going on. I believe there was a connection."

"I guess I'll just have to trust you. But if word of this gets out, my brother may go to jail."

Catherine held up crossed fingers to Harry. "I am very discreet. And I'm not the police."

"Well, a few months back, my brother's name came up in connection with a plot to bomb the Pacific Stock Exchange. Daddy paid hefty bribes to the powers that be—probably the FBI—not to charge Del. If that came out, it could put Daddy and Del in jail. It's a Federal Crime. Daddy was livid with Del, but he covered it all up. Or at least he thought he had. The blackmailer must have known something."

Catherine showed a thumbs-up sign to Harry and grinned

hugely. "You have been a tremendous help, Alvira. I look forward to seeing you in class on Thursday. Am I to meet Lionel?"

"Yes," she said. "He's planning on meeting me after class. But don't bring up the blackmail."

"Of course not. I'll look forward to meeting him."

When she rang off, Harry said, "How clever you are! What was Fields paying blackmail for?"

"Del tried to blow up the Stock Exchange. So much for our ideas of him being a well-behaved little Communist. And his father cut him off months ago. I'll bet you anything that's what the blackmail was about."

"Yes," said Harry, his brows coming together. "But, in that case, why did he stop?"

"Maybe he had something on Buck. About his mysterious past. Maybe that's what he was paying Black to look into."

"Darling, you are positively brilliant!"

Chapter Twenty

Wednesday morning, Catherine woke with the determination to pay another visit to Mr. Phillip Black. Surely he must see that he possessed information in a murder investigation!

Before she could put this plan in action, however, she needed to check on Professor Adler. Catherine rang the hospital.

"Professor Adler passed a peaceful night and is resting comfortably," the nurse on duty told her.

"Wonderful!" said Catherine. She went to find Harry, who was at the diner eating breakfast.

"Dr. Adler is doing well this morning," she told him. She ordered her oatmeal. "And I think we should pay Mr. Black another call. Surely, he must see that he has evidence in a murder investigation."

"I was thinking the same thing. Maybe we can get this case wrapped up today."

The tension in Catherine's neck and shoulders relaxed. "And then I intend to spend some time with Dot. She was asleep when I left the inn."

* * *

They arrived at the detective's office at 10:00. The almost dark staircase took them to the third floor. As soon as they opened the heavy door from the stairwell onto the hall, Catherine noticed the suffocating odor.

"Harry, what is that awful smell?" she asked. "It's like something is rotten, but where can it be coming from?"

They found the office door standing slightly open, and the smell nearly overpowered them.

Harry led her away quickly. "We need to find a telephone," he said. "Something died in there. The other offices on this floor must be empty. No one could miss this smell."

They tried the second floor. An export-import company had its door open.

"I'm calling the police. What was that red-haired detective's name?" Harry asked.

"Davies." Catherine was feeling sick. She had never smelled anything so vile! But it was the idea of what was behind that door that was making her ill.

Harry was back out in the hall moments later. "Davies is on his way. Let's wait for him downstairs."

Catherine heard the siren as the big police car screamed down Figueroa St. What seemed like a split second later, Detective Davies was with them, his bearded partner and a whole crowd of other policemen following.

"Third floor," said Harry. "Follow the smell."

She and Harry were sitting on a padded bench on the ground floor across from a row of closed office doors. Catherine knew if she moved the wrong way, she was going to be sick. She held herself very still, her eyes frantically seeking a ladies' room.

Harry took her hand. "You are green, darling. Take some deep breaths. There's no smell down here."

She did as he suggested, and luckily her nausea began to recede. Harry was pulling his shirt collar away from his neck then drumming his fingers on his knee.

"They must have found something that wasn't the office cat," he said finally. "They've forgotten about us. I'm going up there."

"Are you certain you want to do that?" she asked.

"Darling, I need to tell them why we came. We were right about Phillip Black. The poor guy should have figured out that what he knew made him a target."

"All right," she said, biting her bottom lip.

While Harry was gone, she passed the time by pacing the hallway. If poor Mr. Black was dead, did it really have anything to do with Michael Fields?

Why would it? Fields' murder happened weeks ago. This was just a coincidence.

Waiting for Harry wasn't easy; she had nothing to occupy her but her morbid thoughts.

What if the Fields' murder is connected? Had the detective found something explosive in Buck's background? Why had Buck waited so long to act? Hadn't he figured out that the detective was a danger to him? What had changed? Maybe he had just found out who the detective was who had been hanging around Michael. Perhaps he had only now put the pieces together.

By the time Harry rejoined her, Catherine had already thought of a new course of action.

"It was a horror scene, Catherine," he said. Harry had clearly been running his hands through his usually smooth hair. His movements were jerky, his face stiff. "It's a good thing you didn't see it. Black and his secretary had been shot point-blank—several times each. And with everyone busy elsewhere, I checked the files. The Fields file was empty."

"Do they know when it happened?"

"The medical examiner figures it happened sometime over the weekend."

He ran his hands through his hair again. "I need a drink and a shower. But first, we've got to go back to Fields' office. We must have missed something."

"Yes. I think you'd better skip that shower and drink if we

want to beat the police there," said Catherine. "Did you ever get the film developed?"

"No. I completely forgot. Stupid!"

* * *

By the time they arrived at Michael Fields' apartment, it was 2:30. They made straight for the file cabinet. The divorce evidence was untouched.

"It couldn't be that, could it?"

"Let's look it over again, just to be sure. Maybe Calloway doesn't want his picture taken for some reason."

In addition to all the photographs of Joe Calloway and Mrs. Fields together in compromising positions, there was a report. It proved to be an account of the surveillance details with dates, times, and places.

"I don't see anything about this that would account for murder. And there's still the blackmail to explain."

"Well, let's see what else we have," said Catherine. "Oh, yes. This random report about some guy named Cobb."

Standing next to one another, they read over the 8 ½ by a ten-inch sheet of typewriter paper, titled "RONALD SHIPP COBB."

> *The subject of this investigation was an inmate of the Joliet State Prison from 1919 to 1929. He was imprisoned for several felonies committed in the course of an elaborate fraud. Apparently, Cobb was a very successful "confidence man." He specialized in gaining the trust of wealthy elderly women and defrauding them into "investing" in non-existent companies.*

> *Before his incarceration, the subject resided in an expensive neighborhood in Winnetka on Chicago's North Shore. He preyed upon wealthy widows he met through social clubs. There are a significant number*

*of wealthy widows living on the North Shore. He had
a bogus investment company, whereby he would take
Widow B's money and pay a portion of it in dividends
to Widow A. He had over fifty "clients."*

*Cobb had annual reports and investment prospectuses
printed for twenty different phony companies. His sales
technique involved expensive dinners in downtown
Chicago where the marks would meet "executives"
of his companies. They were treated to gross flattery,
flowers, and "dates" to the symphony where they
would sit in "company boxes."*

*Cobb defrauded these women of a total of fifty thou-
sand dollars.*

*After his release from prison, Cobb disappeared, elud-
ing the parole board completely. His whereabouts has
never been discovered.*

"Crikey," said Catherine. "Here's the goods on someone. He
sounds like a horrible man. Do you suppose it's Buck?

"We'll have to look into his career a bit. See when he came on
the Hollywood scene. But this seems just like a stunt he could pull
off with his looks and manner. And if Fields confronted him with
it, I'm not at all surprised Buck murdered him. And poor, hapless
Mr. Black and his secretary."

"What do we do now?" Catherine asked.

"We'll have to confess to our little adventure in detection and
see that they find this report."

"Let's go back to the inn and call from there. Detective Davies
is not going to be happy, but at least you can get your drink, if
not your shower."

* * *

When they returned to the inn, however, it was to find chaos reigning. Dot was trying to calm Detective Davies, whose red hair was sticking straight up. "Dr. Bascombe? Did you tip off Danforth that we were coming for him?"

"No. I most certainly did not," Harry replied.

"He's taken off. We've got men on the coast roads and on the road to Nevada. He won't get far. He didn't take an airplane."

A small Mexican lady came running into the lounge. Catherine recognized Emma, Daphne's maid. "Oh! Policeman! *Bueno*. You must help. The Señor Buck! He come and take Señorita Binoche! She screams!"

Detective Davies swore roundly and grabbed the telephone in the lounge to call the station and let them know that Danforth had taken a hostage. At the words, Catherine felt as cold as ice.

"Do you know what kind of car Danforth drives?" Davies asked.

"Yes," said Catherine. "He has a black Rolls Royce."

The detective swore. "He might get away from us at that. This is now a kidnapping case. We can call in the FBI. If they're headed for Vegas, the Bureau's agents there can pick them up. Fortunately, Danforth is a well-known figure."

"The FBI?" asked Catherine.

"Federal Bureau of Investigation. They come in on federal crimes—anything that crosses state lines."

Davies was dialing. When he reached the Bureau, he asked for someone named Street. Catherine and Harry listened as he briefly outlined the case against Buck for three murders and Miss Binoche's kidnapping. "We need you on this yesterday," Davies said. "Do us all a favor and get your office in Vegas on this. Also, San Diego and San Francisco. We need this state crawling with agents. If you can cover the railway station, that would be great. I've already got the LAPD looking on the highways."

Catherine was confused by the developments, "Three murders? Whose murder besides the detective and his secretary?"

"Grossman's. The bullet that killed the detective was from the same gun as the one that killed Grossman."

"But how did you find out so quickly?"

"Look, lady, I don't have time for your questions. It's a hunch that I know in my gut will be confirmed. The bullet was the same caliber--.45. From a gun issued in the War. Not too common these days."

She turned to the distraught maid. Catherine thanked Emma for letting them know about Daphne and had the front desk call a taxi for her. She gave the little woman a ten-dollar bill. Emma left the chaos to wait outside for her cab.

Meanwhile, Catherine had been thinking hard. When Davies hung up, she said, "I assume the FBI has agents in Chicago?"

"Of course. It's Gangster City. What's that got to do with any-thing?"

"There's another matter connected to all this . . ."

"Look, lady, save it. I've got my hands full."

There was a small library in the lounge. Absently, she looked over the titles until one of the volumes registered with her. It was *Who's Who in Hollywood.*

She showed it to Harry, and as the policeman was still on the telephone, they took it down to her sitting room.

Catherine looked up Buckingham Danforth. *Really, the man couldn't have given himself a more pretentious stage name.*

The entry was relatively short. Buck hadn't been in any mov-ies during the silent era, so that fit with his possible identity as Ronald Cobb. Catherine read right at the top of the article that he was born in Liverpool, England. Certainly, if he were manu-facturing a personality, he would have chosen a more glamourous place to be born! Liverpool had its share of bully boys, however. No indication in the listing that he had ever spent time in Chicago.

On a whim, she looked up Joseph Daines Calloway. *Born: 1895, Chicago, Illinois.*

She shared the entry with Harry. "And he's just the right age to have been selling trumped-up investments to widows in Chicago in the 1920s!" said Catherine.

Harry said, "The only 'D' is his middle initial. I suppose Fields could have used it as a code to remind him that the cash was for blackmail to Calloway."

"Shall we inform the police?" Catherine asked.

"I think we should find out a bit more first. I don't think the police are going to be too receptive to one more theory at this point," said Harry. "Joe's always at the Starlight. We can see him tonight."

"Not without Buck or Daphne to get us in," said Catherine. "And I just thought of something. Where is the poor professor?"

"He's probably still in the hospital," said Harry. "He's going to be distraught over Daphne."

To their surprise, however, they found the professor relaxing in his room. He was still wearing the oxygen mask, connected to a cylinder by his bed.

He took it off. "What's all the trouble out there?" he asked.

"How're you feeling?" asked Catherine.

"Much stronger, thank you. Why? Has something happened to Daphne?"

Catherine hesitated, but then she saw that the professor was only becoming agitated.

"You have to try to be calm. It appears that Buck has taken Daphne and is trying to escape capture."

"My medicine! Nitroglycerin!" He pointed to the dresser. Catherine went to retrieve it. She remembered her father's heart attack. The professor needed a tablet under his tongue. Without delay, she administered it to him.

After a few moments, Dr. Adler seemed to feel better. "Tell me what is being done," he said.

"They've called in the FBI. They're much better at this sort of thing. They are searching in all directions—both the FBI and the police."

A tear fell down his cheek. "I wish she had never met that man! I wish she had never left France!"

"Well, there's one good thing," said Catherine. "Now that they have a warrant for Buck's arrest for murdering Mr. Fields, they will have to release Daphne from her arrest. She went home to pack for France this morning. She was there when Buck caught up with her."

"Yes. She will be much happier in France. I find that I dislike Hollywood intensely," the professor said.

"As do I, Professor," said Harry.

"Have they checked the ports?" Dr. Adler asked.

Harry swore. "They just mentioned the roads, the railways, and the airports." He made for the door, but he was back again in only a moment. "The police have left. Professor, may I use your telephone?"

Professor Adler said, "Natürlich."

Harry tried the police but couldn't get anyone who was working on the case. Leaving a message that he and Catherine were checking the ports, he hung up.

Chapter Twenty-One

Catherine fetched her hat and sunglasses, and they left after promising the professor they would be very thorough.

"I think we should check San Pedro harbor first," she said to Harry as they sped out of the parking lot, heading for the coast highway. "It's closest."

As they drove through a grove of oilwells, they finally spotted the harbor with its massive ships and turned onto a frontage road. As they got closer, they looked for cruise ships. The only vessels visible were oil tankers and enormous cargo ships. None of them was boarding.

"Let's try Long Beach. I'll bet they have some cruise ships in port. It's Saturday. That's a good day to leave on a cruise," said Catherine.

They found the coast highway again and drove south to Long Beach. In about half an hour, they saw the newer harbor with its many recreational yachts together with large ships. There were two cruise ships—the Mermaid and the Dreamer. Both had their gangplanks out. People were coming and going.

After parking the Chevrolet in one of the lots, they hastened to the Dreamer and boarded its gangplank. A uniformed cruise line employee was waiting at the top.

Catherine smiled at her. "Hello! We've come to say goodbye

to my dear friend Daphne before she sails. Has she boarded yet? Daphne Binoche."

"The movie star? Oh, my goodness. I'm afraid not. I would have remembered her, and I don't have her checked through. Are you sure she was on this ship? We're sailing to Hawaii."

"Oh, how silly of me!" Catherine twittered. "Where is the other ship going?"

"Southampton. England."

"Oh! That's the one. Sorry to have bothered you."

"You'll have to hurry. They're scheduled to depart in half an hour," the woman said.

The Mermaid's horn was blasting as they made their way up another gangplank. Catherine was out of breath. A man in a uniform said that Miss Binoche was on the ship, but it was too late for visitors. They were ready to hoist the gangplank.

Catherine was beside herself. "I simply must see her before she sails. I'm afraid it's a matter of life and death! She is being kidnapped by a murderer!"

"Why are you here then, and not the police?" the man asked, his eyes skeptical.

"Because the FBI and the police are searching the roads, the railway, and the airports!"

"I suggest you have one of those agencies contact the U.S. Coastguard. I'm afraid we have to raise the plank now. You are not ticketed passengers, and so you must leave."

Harry said, "Now see here . . ."

The ship's horn blew again, and the official locked the gate at the top of the gangplank. Harry and Catherine were obliged to hurry down to the dock. "We need a telephone!" he said. "There must be a harbormaster . . ."

They inquired of some sailors they met, but they knew nothing. Finally, they boarded the Dreamer again and asked the cruise line official where the harbormaster was. A little surprised at their request, she indicated a tower to the south.

They virtually ran down the gangplank to the dock and

sprinted to the tower. Entering a white painted door, they climbed the stairs at a rapid pace. Catherine's chest felt like it was on fire, and she was gasping.

Harry, who was in better shape, inquired after the harbormaster, and they were shown to a glass room at the top of the tower. A man in uniform stood looking through mounted binoculars.

"Excuse me, sir," said Harry. "I'm here to report a crime. A friend of ours has just been kidnapped on board the Mermaid. If you will ring the Los Angeles police, they can verify my story. The detective in charge of the case is called Davies. The kidnapped woman is Daphne Binoche."

The harbormaster moved away from his apparatus and looked at them. He had a weathered, wrinkled face and sharp blue eyes. "I will do as you say, but such a thing has never . . . oh, very well."

He put the call through and asked for Detective Davies. Catherine had breath enough to heave a sigh when the man answered.

"Two people are here. They are obviously foreigners, but they are claiming that one of our ships has just departed with a Daphne Binoche who is being kidnapped . . . Yes, yes, yes, sir."

The harbormaster whose eyebrows were invisible beneath his forelock handed the telephone to Harry. Catherine listened as he relayed the situation to the police. He then passed the phone back to the harbormaster.

"Yes, sir. Yes, sir. Right away, sir." Turning to Harry, he said. "I'm calling the Coast Guard. The man dialed another number.

"Harbormaster Grimes, here. The LAPD has a kidnapper and his victim on board the Mermaid bound for England. It is just pulling out of Berth Double C. Stop them. Board the ship and detain Buckingham Danforth. He is holding Miss Daphne Binoche, probably at gunpoint. The police will meet you at the dock."

Catherine and Harry watched as two Coast Guard cutters appeared from nowhere, horns blasting. One maneuvered itself into the Mermaid's channel out ahead so they could be seen by the bridge. They zigzagged back and forth. Using a megaphone, they called upon the ship to return to the dock. The other cutter moved alongside the Mermaid. The vessel was scarcely underway and reversed its direction.

As soon as they were alongside the dock, they threw down the rope ladder, and four Coast Guards boarded. The gangplank was lowered to the deck. Passengers lined the rails witnessing the operation. Harry and Catherine heard the wail of sirens as the police drew near.

"Well, this is a day the passengers won't forget," said Catherine. "Thank you for the bird's-eye view, sir."

"Exactly how do you two come to be involved in this? Isn't Mr. Danforth a movie star?"

"Miss Binoche, another movie star, is a friend," said Harry. "It's a very long story."

"Well, I had better get back to work," the harbormaster said.

"We'll be leaving then."

* * *

As the Coast Guard officers escorted Buck off the boat in handcuffs, Harry and Catherine were not surprised to see photographers had somehow appeared on the scene. Swarms of policemen accompanied Daphne and Buck as they left the Mermaid. The movie stars were put in two separate cars, and to the accompaniment of flashbulbs, they departed from the dock.

"Well, even if Buck didn't do the murders, he's going away for a long time for kidnapping," said Catherine.

"He ran. Don't you think that's an admission of guilt?" Harry asked as they made their way to the car.

"It certainly seems to be. I wish I could relax. I am still uneasy about all of this." Said Catherine. A seagull flew very close, and she dodged. "I'm still bothered by the use of Daphne's gun in the first crime. I know there's an explanation for it, but I just don't think it rings true."

* * *

The professor was so happy that Daphne had been recovered that he cried. The actress would be in with the police for a time while they took her statement, but he insisted on being taken into the station so he would be on hand the moment she was released. Catherine and Harry drove him there in the Chevrolet. They all waited in the foyer of the police department.

When at last, the woman was released, she ran straight to her father and embraced him. "Oh, Papa! I thought I might never see you again!"

"*Liebchen, meine Liebchen,*" the professor murmured into her hair. "*Gottseidank.*"

Daphne murmured back to him in German, tears falling down her lovely face. Catherine's heart warmed at seeing them so joyously reunited. Harry put his arm around her and pulled her against him.

Chapter Twenty-Two

After a few joyous moments, the four of them left the police station and went out to the waiting Chevrolet.

"I have never been so frightened in my life," Daphne said to Catherine and Harry. "Thank you so much for rescuing me. I think Buck has gone completely insane. He held a gun on me the entire time. Even when we were boarding the ship, he had it in his pocket, aimed at me. His chauffeur drove us, so Buck could keep me at gunpoint."

"Kidnapping is a federal crime here, apparently," said Harry. "I don't think he is going to be released from jail for a long, long time."

"He knew he was going to be arrested," Daphne said. "But he kept telling me he was innocent. He took me to bargain with. I was his hostage."

Catherine said, "Yes. You have your maid to thank for your release. She took a taxi to the inn. The police were there speaking to us."

"But it wasn't the police who saved me," Daphne protested. "It was you!"

"It was your father who thought of the ports. No one else gave them a thought. We were concentrating on the roads and the railway and the airports," said Catherine as Harry drove through the streets of LA.

"Where would you like to go, Daphne? To your house or to the inn?"

"Papa, will you come with me to the house? I want you beside me while I pack up. The movie will be canceled for certain now. I am going back to France as soon as possible."

If that is your wish, *Liebchen.*"

* * *

When they finally made it back to the inn, they found Richard Darcy waiting for them.

"Here are the heroes of the hour! You are tremendous! I insist that you come to my house tonight for a grand celebration. It will be the event of the year in Hollywood!"

How could they turn him down? He was bursting with good cheer.

"I know you are probably worn out from your efforts, but my party won't begin 'til after my broadcast, so you have plenty of time to rest. I will expect you at 9:30. There will be food and plenty of drinks!

* * *

Dot and Max descended upon them before Catherine and Harry were able to escape to their rooms. They had to hear the entire episode.

"So, are you convinced of Buck's guilt?" Dot asked.

"No. At least not in the matter of Fields' death. But you know what's awfully weird? It appears that both Grossman and Fields went to Phillip Black for the same reason. They were both being blackmailed and wanted some dirt of their own on the black-mailer. And they chose the same detective!"

"It's really not all that odd," said Harry. "While I was in Black's office with the police this morning, they told me that Black was the best in the business. And when you think of the job he did, uncovering Cobb, he must have been good."

"Oh. Well, that makes sense then."

"Are you two ready for a grand Hollywood party tonight?" Catherine asked. "Richard Darcy is throwing it. We're the guests of honor, so I'm sure we can bring our cheering section."

"Crickey!" said Dot.

* * *

Catherine was entirely too wound up to nap. Instead, she lost herself in *The Great Gatsby*, wondering how many successful Gatsbys there were in Hollywood. Was Buck one? How about Joseph Calloway? Hollywood was a phenomenon—a society unlike any other.

Could it ever have arisen anywhere other than America? Nowhere in Europe certainly. Musing on these ideas, she finally did manage to nod off into a pleasant slumber.

She woke at 6:00. The quartet of friends enjoyed a relaxed dinner at the diner, and then Dot and Catherine helped one another do their hair. It was nice to have some help for a change.

Harry, who was following the news on the wireless, came in to inform them that experts had indeed confirmed that the same gun had shot Black, his secretary, and Grossman. Inquiries were being made into Buck's life during the decade that Cobb was in prison. Catherine awaited those developments with interest.

She and Dot took their time applying makeup, and her friend was full of multiple Max anecdotes

"I guess I just have a weakness for cowboys," Dot confessed.

"I'd say that's putting it mildly," Catherine said with a laugh.

* * *

Richard Darcy's Hollywood mansion put all the others she had seen to shame. It was a small castle with turrets. The guests wore their finest apparel, and the food was lavish and delicious. Catherine was glad to see Hyacinth there.

"Who would have thought Buck would kill all those people!" the actress said. "He was a pain and a snob, but I didn't ever think he was a killer!"

"Could we talk about the night Herr Grossman was killed? You'll probably have to testify at the trial. I assume he never hinted that the blackmailer was Buck?

"No. Helmut never told me who it was. Just that it was someone with lots to hide, and he was going to 'nail him to the wall' like I said."
. A little later in the evening, Lady Naomi found her.

"Congratulations again on your screen test," Catherine said. "What's the next step?"

"I spoke to Buck's agent today. He's going to take me on. It was the most wonderful piece of luck."

"I'm happy for you," Catherine said truthfully.

The woman turned to her, her eyes keen. "You're not really serious about Harry Bascombe, are you?"

Catherine narrowed her eyes. "What business is that of yours?"

"Just sisterly affection. You could do so much better, you know," Lady Naomi said with a superior smile. "You're Baron Tregowyn's daughter, right? The poet?"

"Harry suits me down to the ground," said Catherine, her voice cool.

The subject of their conversation approached and asked them, "May I get you ladies a drink?"

"Gin and tonic for me, thanks," said the aspiring actress.

"Plain tonic for me, darling. Thank you," said Catherine.

"It's a tremendous shame about poor Buck. What a perfectly horrid waste of a grand man," said Lady Naomi. She glided off like a ship with all flags flying.

* * *

The inevitable time arrived when Catherine needed to repair to the loo. She asked a passing servant where she should go.

"Oh," the woman in her black uniform said. "You'll have to use the one upstairs. We are having some problems with the one down here. It's down the hall to the right at the top of the stairs."

Catherine found her way down a labyrinthian hall with passages. After she had powdered her nose, she found herself turned around, unable to remember which route to take back to the stairs. Turning to the right, she walked a short distance, enjoying the pictures on the wall of her host in front of various iconic landmarks in Hollywood—the Brown Derby, Grauman's Chinese Theater, and the Beverly Wilshire. At the end of the hall, there was a picture of a much younger Darcy. He was standing on a sailboat deck grinning, his arm around a happy blonde woman. She wondered how long ago it was taken. The boat's stern proclaimed it to be *The Bonnie Lass* from Chicago. At first, she smiled at the young Richard Darcy, but then she realized the picture's significance, and her stomach became a cold pit.

Chicago. Richard Darcy. "D." Ronald Cobb. Why on earth did he have it hung, even in this out-of-the-way place?

Head spinning, Catherine turned to walk back the way she came and ran into the picture's subject. He looked from her to photo and back again. The normally genial man's nostrils flared, and his jaw set tightly. He knew she knew.

Startled, Catherine said, "Mr. Darcy! I'm afraid I've become lost. Which way to the stairs?"

His friendly mask back in place, he gave a short laugh. "Sorry. It's a bit confusing up here—one of the disadvantages of a castle."

She laughed but felt cold inside. Catherine knew she must find Harry. However, her host was disposed to linger.

"Do you play chess?" he asked, effectively blocking her way. "I have rather a marvelous chess set in here." He opened a door.

"Sorry," she said, forcing a smile. "I've never learned."

"It's time for you to do so now." Grabbing her arm, the man

pushed her into the room. "I'm afraid my greatest flaw is my vanity."

Catherine stumbled and landed on the floor. Darcy closed the door, and she heard the big lock turn on the outside.

She pounded the floor in frustration. Her stomach quivered in fear. Catherine stood and groped her way in the darkness to the light switch. A beautifully carved marble chess set did sit on a table in the middle of the room. Heavy velvet drapes blotted out the night. There was no furniture except two chairs pulled up to the table.

Catherine drew back the drapes. As she had hoped, there was a small balcony. The French door to the outside was locked, but it was a heavy, old-fashioned kind of lock. Removing her gloves, she took the ornate knight off the chess table, working its brass spear loose until she held it in her hand.

As she moved to the door, she noted vaguely that she had begun to perspire all over. Catherine worked the knight's long jousting spear into the lock on the door. Poking it around carefully, she managed, after precious lost minutes, to tease open the locking mechanism. She threw her tool on the floor and eased the French door wide.

Catherine stood on the narrow balcony looking around her. The drop to the ground was too long as the ridiculous castle had a moat, though it was dry. She looked up. The castle walls were constructed of rough stones. If she could manage to climb them, there was a possibility she could reach the roof above the next story. Kicking off her shoes, she took the hem of her gown in her hands and tore the flimsy fabric up the sides all the way to her torso on both sides.

Catherine was not without experience. There were many authentic castle ruins in her neighborhood in Cornwall. She and her brother had made sport of climbing such walls when they were children.

Standing on the balcony rail, she grabbed the stones above her and thanked Providence that they were rough and not smooth.

Catherine stepped off the rail one foot at a time, finding purchase for her feet on the stones. Carefully, she moved her right foot and hand higher, found her grip, and then moved higher, scaling the wall carefully until she reached the balcony above her.

With only a fragile hope, she tested that French door and found it locked as well. Once again, she took to the castle walls with her hands and feet. This time, she made it all the way up. She grabbed a stone ornament sitting on the battlements, but it was loose, and she nearly fell. Once she had steadied herself, she gripped the balustrade and pulled herself up and over the battlements to the roof. Catherine took a deep breath and congratulated herself.

A narrow shelf lay between the battlements and the roof, just wide enough for her to walk on. Her hands and feet bled from the stones' roughness, but she hurried on, walking the top of the castle, searching for the staircase that would take her down. Squinting in the darkness, Catherine finally found a set of steps leading down the back wall. At last, she was down on the ground!

The Chevrolet would be challenging to find in the dark. She walked over the lawn to the meadow where the cars were parked and squinted to see the familiar outlines of their black hired car. They had arrived early. Therefore she knew it would be parked in the back of the meadow. How was she going to find Harry? Would he be taken, too?

She decided that the best plan would be for her to go straight to the police. She hadn't driven on the right side of the road in Chevrolet. But she couldn't let that hold her back now! The keys would be in the ignition as a valet had parked the car.

Catherine finally located it. Slipping in behind the wheel, she maneuvered herself with difficulty until she was out of the meadow and on the road. The Bel Air road could have been in the midst of the country; it was so dark. She could scarcely see.

When she finally made her way out to Wilshire Boulevard, she mistakenly turned down the street going the wrong way. In less than an instant, she heard a siren and saw flashing lights in her rearview mirror.

* * *

There was absolutely nothing she could do to convince the traffic policeman that she wasn't drunk. She also had no driving license with her. He put her in handcuffs and gave her a ride down to the police station. Other policemen impounded the Chevrolet.

"If you just telephone Detective Davies, he will confirm who I am. It's imperative that I talk to him as soon as possible. This is a murder case!"

"I don't know where you've been keeping yourself, ma'am. Detective Davies solved that murder case today. A real-life Hollywood actor is in Lincoln Fields. I'm not gonna be the one to wake Davies and tell him some crazy drunk broad is down here screaming murder!"

The cell door clanged shut. Catherine went to the smelly bunk in the corner and sank down, head in her hands. Harry was going to be alarmed. He would probably call the police to report her missing. What a comedy of errors!

And adding to everything was the fact that her scraped-up hands and feet were killing her. She couldn't even imagine how filthy the floor of the jail must be.

When he discovered she was gone, would Darcy run? She thought he would.

* * *

Catherine judged it would take Harry about two hours to decide to get back to the inn once he discovered her and the Chevrolet gone. The police said she had one telephone call. She used it to call Harry, hoping he'd be waiting.

"Darling!" he answered once the front desk had put him through. "Where the devil are you?"

"I'm at the police station downtown. In jail! I have a lot to tell you. Will you please get Mr. Westerman and come down here?

I was arrested for drunk driving, trying to escape from Darcy. I have a lot to tell, and the police won't listen."

Fortunately, Harry knew it was time for action and not more questions. "We'll be there as quickly as we can."

* * *

She had never been so happy to see Harry. He tried to grab her hands through the jail's bars, but she winced.

"What have you done to yourself?" he demanded.

"It's a long story. We need to get Detective Davies! I'm sure Darcy is getting away now that he realizes I've escaped!"

"We'll have to leave it up to Westerman to explain, I think. Where are your shoes? Why is your dress torn?"

"All right. I'll tell you. I climbed up the castle wall to the roof. Darcy had me locked in a room. I found a picture of him standing on a boat with the home port of Chicago! Davies needs to get that boat registration! Darcy is Ronald Shipp Cobb! Not Buck! He killed Fields, and Grossman, and Black."

"The devil he did!"

Chapter Twenty-Three

Mr. Westerman managed to convince the police that Catherine had had nothing to drink, that she was genuinely involved in the murder case, and that her claims were to be taken seriously. He took the initiative to call Detective Davies at his home.

The news that Catherine had been locked in a room in the castle after recognizing an old picture of Darcy on a boat in Chicago was enough to convince Davies to send out an All Points Bulletin for the man. Surmising his fondness for boats, the Coast Guard was called to check all the marinas while the police covered the roads, airports, and train stations.

When morning came, the policeman put a call into the Chicago police. By afternoon, they had the information that the *The Bonnie Lass* in the picture was registered to Ronald Cobb. A search of the castle revealed the gun that had killed Grossman, Black, and his secretary.

Meanwhile, Harry took Catherine to the emergency room, where the wounds on her hands and feet were tended to. Dot wanted to fuss over her, but Catherine insisted on returning to Police Headquarters so they could follow the chase for Cobb.

Catherine felt so helpless. If only she had been able to raise the alarm right away!

Davies called in the FBI to carry out the search across state lines. Catherine was running on pure adrenaline, and Harry stayed right at her side. The Coast Guard had determined that "Darcy" had another sailboat registered to him, here in California. This one was called *Lizzie*. Harry caught on to the irrelevant fact that Cobb/Darcy must be a *Pride and Prejudice* fan.

In late afternoon, the Coast Guard caught the *Lizzie* in the waters off San Diego, presumably making for Mexico. They arrested Cobb on four counts of murder and the much smaller matter of parole violation. This time, Ronald Shipp Cobb was not going to get released from prison. And California was a death penalty state.

* * *

Catherine felt herself to be a truant after missing Thursday's class, but she did manage to make her lecture on the War Poets on Friday night. The room was crowded to bursting. Harry read the best of the age's heart-wrenching poetry to loud applause.

She felt Darcy/Cobb's absence keenly. He had undoubtedly been a thorough confidence trickster. He had fooled them all with his enthusiasm and his bonhomie. If he only hadn't taken to murder . . .

Daphne stayed with her father at the inn that night. As soon as he was well enough, they would travel back to Europe in a leisurely manner by cruise ship. The actress was watching her father's health like a hawk.

Saturday morning, the Adlers took Catherine and Harry out for brunch to show their gratitude for all their new friends had done for them.

"You are on your way back to France?" asked Catherine. "Poor Hollywood. What a loss you will be."

"I don't think I am suited for the Hollywood life," said Daphne. "I will leave it to Lady Naomi. I predict that she will make a great success."

"And you, Professor?" asked Catherine.

"I was able to break my contract with the university because of my health. I will spend some time in France, near to Dafna, until she is on her feet again. Then I go back to Vienna."

"There is no way we can adequately thank you for all you have done for us. I hope the rest of your month is very much calmer," said Daphne.

"We were glad to help," said Catherine, realizing that over the past couple of weeks, she had come to like Daphne. "We wish you the most tremendous success in Paris."

* * *

By the time they arrived at the cliffs and shores of Laguna that afternoon, Catherine felt like she was coming out of a dream. Wearing her sunglasses and a large hat, she got out of the car with Harry's help, and they began their descent down to Diver's Cove. Since her feet were bandaged, she needed to keep her shoes on even in the sand.

She was going to miss the seashore when they went back to Oxford. As they walked through the sand, they rounded a lava rock formation that projected from the cliffs and came to another stretch of beach. They didn't say much, and Catherine allowed the salt spray to cool her and clear her thoughts.

Harry pulled her close to him, and she savored his presence as they progressed toward another outcropping. When they arrived, they were enchanted to find tide pools.

"Look, there are starfish!" Catherine cried. And those round spikey things."

"I believe those are sea anemones," said Harry. Using a piece of driftwood, he poked the organism, and it closed on itself. There were many other sea creatures they couldn't name. A large wave came in and flooded their little pool.

"That's you, darling. I told you you're like a tidal wave. And you've done it."

"Done what?" he asked, grinning.

"Made me fall in love with you."

Putting his hands on her shoulders, he said, "You're certain?"

"I am. It's taken me long enough to admit it, hasn't it?"

Reaching down into the pool for a sand dollar, he handed it to her. "To remember this day," he said. His eyes were fixed on hers, and she saw the tenderness there. Despite a small audience of crabs and starfish, they kissed hungrily. At that moment, she felt their passion possessed the strength and turbulence of the incoming waves.

Catherine shut her eyes and held on to Harry for dear life. She had done it! She had committed herself aloud. But now that she had done it, she thought that Harry had known it all along.

* * *

"Well, well," said Max. "I don't suppose you're ready for some good news?"

"Always," said Catherine.

"I'll be joining you at Oxford again if they'll have me in a post-grad program at one of the colleges," Max said. "And this time, I'm going to bring my cowboy hat and boots."

As he kissed Dot on the cheek, her friend beamed and blushed.

"This is wonderful news!" said Catherine. "We will welcome your coming back to Oxford, Max!"

"We have some ground-breaking news, as well," said Harry, settling his arm around Catherine's shoulder.

"Do tell!" said Dot.

"Harry has asked me to marry him, and I've said yes," Catherine said. "We are thinking about a Christmas wedding."

Dot squealed in a most un-British sort of way. "Spiffing!" she declared. "Absolutely spiffing."

"Definitely spiffing," said Harry, leaning over to kiss his fiancée on the lips. "I think perhaps champagne is in order."

THE END

Acknowledgements

Writing a book during COVID 19 was difficult. When I thought I was finished, my daughter read it and said, "Mom! This isn't you! What happened?" It had been tough to write, but I didn't know how horrible it was! She spent days of her scarce time (she was homeschooling five kids because of aforesaid COVID 19) making a list of things I needed to change! It was a huge relief for me to realize what was wrong!

As usual, this book was plotted mainly by my husband David and me while sitting in The Corner Bakery. We start out with index cards and invent characters. Then we follow the characters through the story they are making. I am very grateful to him for all his great ideas and for all the fun we have!

Other Books by G.G. Vandagriff

Catherine Tregowyn Mysteries
An Oxford Murder
Murder in the Jazz Band
Murder at Tregowyn Manor
Murder in Hollywood
*

Romantic Suspense
Breaking News
Sleeping Secrets
Balkan Echo
*

Historical Fiction
The Last Waltz: A Novel of Love and War
Exile
Defiance
*

Women's Fiction
Pieces of Paris
The Only Way to Paradise
*

Genealogical Mysteries
Cankered Roots
Of Deadly Descent
Tangled Roots
Poisoned Pedigree
Hidden Branch
*

Suspense
Arthurian Omen
Foggy With a Chance of Murder
*